SKIES OF

SKIES O.

MW00583432

An Isle of Write Anthology

Edited by John Appel, Mary Alexandra
Agner, and Jo Miles

1

Introduction and Foreword

IT STARTED, AS SO MANY things do, as a joke.

At some point back in the winter or spring of 2017, a number of us on the Slack community Isle of Write bounced around the idea of putting together an anthology—a group project, for fun. People started bouncing themes around until someone said "Airships!"

"No, airship pirates!"

"Wait! Airship pirate wizards!"

Silly? Maybe. Ridiculous? Kinda. But the idea stuck with us, and off and on through the summer of 2017 the idea would bubble up again and again. We'd hash it over, sometimes toying with other themes, but we kept coming back to this one. The world might be on fire, but we were drawn to respond in the way writers and other creative people do in such times: by making art, and making it with our friends.

A number of us were together in person at ReaderCon in July 2017 and the subject came up once more. Somewhere between our Saturday night room party and breakfast Sunday morning I decided this needed to become reality, and offered to organize the project. Jo Miles and Mary Agner immediately volunteered to assist; several of the writers whose stories follow said they were in as contributors; and thus we embarked on the journey which brought this collection together.

Herein you'll find a baker's dozen stories of daring feats and breathtaking action, of heart-wrenching choices, of families formed and families broken, stories of love and loss and victory. You'll meet golems, werewolves, and a wide array of both wizards and pirates. So grab your cutlass or wand, climb aboard, and set sail for Skies of Wonder, Skies of Danger.

The Adventure of the Unburnt Book

by Tyler Hayes

WHEN ENGAGING IN THE high-risk, high-reward career of airborne book piracy, precise planning is not the asset many think; the very nature of the world after the Time Crash makes timing fluid at best and physics a matter of debate. Rather, flexibility is paramount, the capacity to keep wits intact and paradigm-shifters ready for the inevitable moment when one's plan goes awry. Unfortunately, flexible thinking can create problems just as easily as it can escape them, which is how we ended up grappled to a ship that had just caught fire.

The trap should have been obvious. The capture of the airship *Little Free Library* was the most massive blow struck by the Reich Eternal since they burned the Elder Library; an entire ship dedicated to spreading the written word, taken out of the air by soldiers dedicated to its destruction. Not only that, I and the rest of the *Logophile*'s crew were superstars of the Luftwaffe bounty rolls. Beth, our resident wizard, dared to be successful while Jewish; Ambrose, the undead dragon skull in the hold, lived on the very books the Literary Hygiene Division sought to purge; and the Nazis knew me as the Book Golem, the monster who refused to burn down with his library, a stone monster in a blurry video, decimating an LGA flamethrower team. The Nazis had been stamping out our legend everywhere we went, going so far as to bulldoze an entire print shop just because they printed a newspaper with us in it.

That the Nazis would go to great lengths to defend their prize was a given; that we were expected was a foregone conclusion; but we failed to consider book-burners would escalate to burning a whole ship just to catch us in the flames. And yet, within a few minutes of our grapple-lines dragging the *Library* out of their air fortress, when it was far too late to cut it loose, the *Library* ignited, with a whoosh of combusting air I could hear from belowdecks. I stopped setting up for my penmanship practice, my stomach sinking as I realized our flawless, daring rescue was to be far more of the latter than the former.

Beth, ever the frontline leader, insisted she would handle the problem.; She accelerated, shouting the sea-shanties that powered the *Logophile*'s engines, trying to combine escape and extinguishing by letting the wind douse the flames. But the wind only fed the conflagration, and with Ambrose's panicked shrieks of "Save the books!" commandeering our radios, I put aside my pencil––why waste our scant paper when my cursive wasn't coming along anyway?––and ran abovedecks, where Beth and I found ourselves clipping onto the grapple-lines and plunging toward the deck of the *Library* below, looting bags in hand.

As I slid down the cables toward a ship engulfed in brilliant emerald flames, the heat conjuring images of the Elder Library, I was sure I had reached the apex of my capacity for fear. But even my old trauma did not prepare me for what awaited us belowdecks. Everything about the *Little Free Library*, from the overstuffed chairs to the polish on the bookshelves, was dedicated to the love of books, and by the time I was seeing it, it was already beyond hope.

"Can you save the books?" Ambrose shouted over the radio. The trouble with Ambrose is that the line between "books for everybody" and "the hoard he needs to survive" is malleable at best.

Beth looked at our two simple oilskin bags and into one of the dozen cabins, every shelf laden with books. The grim set of her jaw said all that needed to be said.

"Cap," I grunted. When I had her attention, I signed "I'll take the ones already on fire." Sign language worked far better than speech––a mouth of clay leaves something to be desired when paired with a brain of sacred geometry.

Beth pointed me to the most consumed of the cabins, produced a sphere of sapphire from her coat, and recited the opening verse to "Hallelujah." The crystal glowed as her paradigm shifted to accommodate its workings.

"Stay cool, brother mine," she said as the crystal shielded her in glittering ice.

The flames didn't affect my body, but that didn't make them any less damaging; the first books I saw upon entering were already on their way to ashes. At first I grabbed any tome that remained unscathed, but before I even left the first room my bag was starting to bulge. I charged through the next door and stood, paralyzed, as I tried to decide which books most needed to be brought back to safety.

Before I took up piracy, my purpose was to guard the Elder Library at New Cambridge; I was quite literally built to believe in the inherent value of the book. I would not judge a copy of *Superfudge* any less worthy than *Moby Dick*, and neither would triumph over a Sedaris essay; every story is the key to a long-locked door for someone. So to pass wall after wall of books, weighing them not only by psychic impact but by mass and dimensions, was to take an entrenching tool to my soul. But listening to the roaring fire, thinking of my first home, I knew this was my burden to bear. I dove into the flames, and I saved what I could; and as my reward, my radio gave me news I didn't want to hear.

"Hello?" asked a deep, feminine-sounding voice.

I hesitated to respond, given my difficulties with speech.

Beth took up the cause for me. "This is Captain Beth Kaplan of the *Logophile*. Who is this?"

The speaker responded with thanks to God in the language of my youth. "This is Captain Sayyida al-Hurra of the *Little Free Library*. We're in danger."

"We're onboard your ship," Beth said. "Have you been taken prisoner?" In her voice I heard the same shameful hope I felt: that we might continue our plunder before devoting time to a rescue.

"We're in the hold!" the woman cried. "Please, the hatch is stuck––we––" The punctuation to her plea was the crack of collapsing timber.

I didn't need to see Beth to know her mind. We'd discussed this scenario many times; saving books was our calling, but books didn't matter if no people were around to read them.

"We're coming to get you," Beth said.

All around me I could hear the books burning, pages curling under the onslaught of the heat. Still, I met Beth in the passageway, and found us a ladder. Beth darted down and ran ahead of me, gasping words of reassurance into the radio when she had breath to spare.

We found the hold by following the black snakes of smoke curling along the orlop deck. The hatch was pinned in place by a stack of flaming timbers from the collapsed ceiling above, the epicenter of a spreading blaze. Beth kept me from charging forward while she whispered part of "Wichita Vortex Sutra." As she spoke, the ice crystals surrounding her shot into the heart of the fire. The ice struggled at first, but a few more snatches of Ginsberg and the ice's paradigm won out over the fire's, leaving only a patch of scorched wood.

"You can come out now," Beth called as she opened the hatch.

Two people took tentative steps into our field of vision. One was human, feminine, a sunburnt face beneath a red silk hijab; the other looked feminine by human standards but was as much piscine as primate, with glittering silver skin and gills fluttering at their neck, dressed in a long blue tunic and a mantle that looked like an entire dire wolf hide. Both looked at us with understandable suspicion.

"Captain al-Hurra?" Beth asked, saluting. "Captain Kaplan. Call me Beth. She/her/hers."

The one in the hijab returned the salute with stiff, stilted movements. "Sayyida. She/her/hers. This is––"

"Sigrunn," the fish-person said, still uncertain. "Same."

Beth turned to me. "And this is––"

There was a snap overhead, and the colossal whoosh of another flaming timber falling from above. I lunged forward and caught the beam before it could plunge through the hatch;

Sayyida looked at me in amazement and gratitude, and I answered back with a smile.

"Cragg," Beth said. "He/him/his."

Beth beckoned them upward, watching the ceiling with great concern. Sayyida only made the ascent with help from Sigrunn.

"You're wounded," Beth said.

Sayyida flinched, ashamed. "I am so sorry," she said. "When the fascists captured us, we saw them start to bring the chemicals onboard––we'd heard the stories, tried to––" Sayyida cut off with a hiss of pain.

Sigrunn spoke over the gap in the apology. "We tried to fight. They cut Sayyida, took her hostage while they loaded in their Greek fire."

Beth scowled. "We'll do the best we can to save––"

"Friends?" said Ambrose over the radio, urgency galvanizing his words. "We're about to be boarded!"

We all buckled inside at the news. Beth gave me a bleak look as she answered. "Sitrep, please."

"I have one Reich frigate inbound. They're carrying Untotsoldaten, but...I cannot tell how many. Let me see––a frigate––there could be as many as four hundred––"

If before we buckled, under this news we broke. Untotsoldaten, the Reich Eternal's jetpack zombies: quick, unfeeling, relentless. And as many as four hundred?

Beth closed her eyes, lips moving in rapid-fire whispers as she tried to formulate a plan. Sayyida looked at Sigrunn, both despairing. I nudged Beth, and signed "reassurance" to her.

"We won't leave you behind," Beth declared to the two *Library* crew members. "Everyone lives. Except Nazis."

Burning wood popped somewhere above us, as if in defiance of Beth's resolve. Sayyida looked at Sigrunn; something passed between them that left Sayyida nodding insistently and Sigrunn shaking her head.

"Sayyida, no––"

"I'm already too wounded to stand and fight, Sigrunn," Sayyida said. "Plus, I have the better sense of self-preservation." She turned away as though the argument were settled. "Captain Kaplan, I am going to stay behind. I want to do something rash."

Beth smirked. "Does this rash undertaking have the potential to ruin some Nazis' days?"

"If it works," Sayyida replied with a similar expression.

Beth nodded, and to my fright, unclipped the carabiner from her belt and handed it to Sigrunn. "Rashness is easier with two pairs of hands."

Before I could ask a question, Beth turned and wrapped me in a tight hug. Her voice did not waver as she told me, "Take care of the ship, brother. I'll be back soon."

Behind us, Sayyida and Sigrunn shared a long, desperate kiss. Sigrunn was slow to let go of her captain, but Sayyida was patient, whispering reassurances and wiping away tears until she detached.

"I'm so angry at you," Sigrunn said.

"I love you, too," Sayyida replied.

We split up on the spot, Sayyida directing Beth toward the engine room, explaining her plan in wrathful tones.

"Do you ever feel like your captain's sidekick?" Sigrunn asked me as we made our ascent.

I was embarrassed at how I had to respond. "Words...bad. Mouth...clay."

We climbed up onto the deck, Sigrunn in the lead. She craned her neck to gaze past the *Library*'s masts, glowering at what she saw. "Doesn't look like talking is the order of the day anyway."

The Reich frigate hovered in the air above us, a sleek, sharp thing made of pitch-black wood, throbbing with the sickly green light of the necromantic runes that kept it aloft. Leaping overboard and heading for the *Logophile* were scores of dark figures in brown uniforms, each one's path traced by a chemical blue blaze from the jetpack that bore them through the air.

My radio clicked to life––Ambrose, declaring in a fragile calm, "We're boarded. I'm guarding the deck with all the ectoplasm I can muster, but these abominations will overrun my defenses with great alacrity."

Sigrunn turned to me. "Does your ship have any other defenses?"

"Me," I said.

Sigrunn grinned, and said something melodious in a language that sounded like Old Norse. A sword appeared in her outstretched hand, a long, gray blade in the Viking style, lightning crackling along its edges.

"And me," she said, and clipped herself to one of the grapple-lines.

I followed suit, and we ascended, the lines jiggling under our weight, the looting bag swaying heavily in my hand. I watched the Untotsoldaten leaping onto our ship, sabers at the ready, and felt rage boiling into my extremities.

"Shield...ship," I said to Sigrunn. "Bring...here."

"I was thinking the same thing," declared Sigrunn, who brandished her sword and shouted what sounded like a prayer to Odin.

It had the desired effect; several zombies swung their decaying heads toward us and did an about-face, their hunger for the living overriding their master's commands. I clasped the line hard with my thighs and made my free hand into a fist as the jetpack zombies jetted toward us.

Untotsoldaten are strong, enduring, and without mercy. But they are also incapable of more than the most basic, blood-lust-tinged thoughts; so when they tried to join us in combat, the first two broke their swords uselessly against my stone skin, only for their faces to meet my unrelenting stone fist. Black helmets tumbled down, followed by the rest of the now-inert corpses.

Next to me, Sigrunn kept climbing, chanting her Old Norse paradigm-shifter, swinging her sword in great arcs that brought with them gale-force winds. Zombies scattered before her onslaught, spinning out of control in the tempest, and those that managed to engage her found a spirited combatant; limbs and helms sloughed off around her like waves breaking against a ship.

Sixty feet of open air remained between us and the *Logophile*; we ascended as fast as we could under the assault. Fifty-five feet from the deck, Sigrunn stopped to duel two zombies. At fifty feet, I dispatched one with an uppercut, another with a headbutt. At forty-five feet, one produced a pistol with enough paradigm to fire; I shielded Sigrunn from the bullets, and she summoned a biting wind that sent the monster skidding away. And all around us, zombies rained down from the *Logophile*, their jetpacks stripped away by Ambrose's powers. I felt exultant, alive, grateful for this new companion and this chance to bloody the Reich's nose, some small recompense for the books already destroyed.

My life has often turned on ironies.

We were halfway to the ship. I struck the latest zombie a glancing blow; it gripped my throat, smashing its saber against my shoulder, cracking and denting me even as it ruined its weapon. I gripped it with my free hand, and unthinking, gleeful at victory, I clouted the zombie across the head with my looting bag. The creature fell away from my grasp, and the tip of its saber came up with inexorable speed and dug deep into the bottom of my bag, ripping the oilskin wide open.

Books tumbled free of the bag, dropping out of reach before I could react: two, three, four of them, all lost to the sky. I lashed out an elbow to drive the zombie back, and squeezed the bag tight in both hands, clutching the remaining books to my chest. Sigrunn saw me defenseless and summoned another gale, sending the zombie spiraling away. Losing books again stung, but another peril loomed larger: the bag required two hands now. I had no way to climb, fight, and keep the books safe.

I looked at the zombies swarming down at us, trying to think of a way to get a moment's respite, just a moment. I hit upon a plan, but enacting it would require...

"Fish!" I yelled, already mortified.

Sigrunn glared at me.

"Ray...dee...talk box!" I was grateful I could not blush.

Sigrunn, scribes be praised, understood. She reached out and pressed Send on my radio.

"Skull!" I yelled at the device. "Skull!"

"Cragg!" replied Ambrose. "I'm here!"

"Dan-ger!" I shouted. "Dan-ger! Need...dis...dis..." I scowled.

Sigrunn gave me an apologetic frown, and pulled the radio closer to her. "We need a distraction!"

"Who is this?" demanded Ambrose.

"Now!" replied Sigrunn.

Ambrose did not respond verbally; but after a moment, there came an unearthly wail from above us, and a wave of ghastly, green, ragged sheets of paper lashed out from the deck of the *Logophile*, cascading into the side of the black frigate. Ambrose's spectral assault dissipated against the runes warding the enemy ship, but it was enough to make a plurality of the zombies turn their attention to matters higher up than us.

Two stray zombies still scudded toward our position. I held onto my prize and the rope, letting Sigrunn take the initiative while I tried to solve our problem. There were too many books to carry by hand; the bag was too full and too damaged to tie off the bottom. The grapple-lines were already igniting below us, so simply hanging here and weathering the attack would be impossible even if the *Logophile* were not in danger. The zombies' jetpacks ran off who-knew-what paradigm, rendering them as useful as lead weights. The Elder Library flashed into my mind, its books disintegrating, my creators screaming...not again, no, not again...

"There's too many!" Ambrose broadcast. "I do not know how long I can hold them!"

An idea took shape in my head and was banished three separate times before I let it gain purchase. I looked at the books I was clutching and took stock.

Again, the pain of trying to rank the value of books. But Ambrose was fifty feet above us, besieged; and Beth was below, risking life and limb on the plan of a total stranger. How could I do anything less?

Fate chose that moment to pile more straw atop our backs. Sigrunn swung into me, pushing off me to lunge out and skewer an oncoming zombie. She pendulumed back toward me, beheaded another rocketing in from port——and as she recovered, a third zombie came in from above and caught her a vicious slash across her off-hand side. Blood streamed from the wound, and the moment of pain slowed Sigrunn's counterattack, allowing the creature to follow through with a left hook that stunned the fishwoman enough to send her skidding back down the grapple-line.

Thought and strategy gave way to haste. I struck the zombie a haymaker blow that sent its skull flying——joined by two of the books. I let myself fall, my body pivoting about the point where my thighs clenched the line, and stretched my hand out to the falling Sigrunn. She caught my wrist, then gasped in horror as books came avalanching out of the torn bag; she reached out her sword hand to lend support, but by the time we had the bag stable, we were supporting all of a half-dozen volumes.

We hung there, spinning in space, me upside-down, Sigrunn hanging from one hand, the gashed bag of books from the other. I looked at Sigrunn, dangling a lethal distance above the burning *Library*; I looked at the books, the only survivors of that inferno, barely held in place by our two hands. Even if I did not have to help her, even if her wound did not diminish her mobility, I needed to turn myself right side up again...

"Need...grab...rope," I said.

Sigrunn's eyes were wild. "If we don't save the books, they'll have taken everything from us."

I hated myself as I answered. "You...first." I closed my eyes, a moment of quiet before I had to say it. "Will...take...one."

Sigrunn's black eyes bulged, but she set her lip and nodded.

I looked inside the bag, at what remained of our ill-fated haul. We had a collection of horror stories by an award-winning author. We had a signed first edition of a seminal mystery novel. We had an atlas of Europe circa World War IV, a kraken-skin journal with a scant few entries, and a Congolese classic so old the binding had been replaced with everseal tape. I looked at each of them, mind spinning at the words I would never read. With my stomach in my throat, I made my choice.

I brought the bag closer to my mouth and bit down as hard as I could manage on the kraken-skin journal. I shook my head, making sure a quick worrying did not loosen the book from my mouth. And then we let the rest fall.

They plummeted like stones. Their pages ripped free in the wind; their bindings collapsed as they lost their insides; their lavish covers flipped end over end, back toward the very place we'd tried to rescue them from. I closed my eyes, and I said goodbye.

Her sword hand freed, Sigrunn gripped the line below me. I helped her climb up closer to me and wrapped my arm around her waist, supporting her weight in lieu of her damaged abdominal muscles. She smiled, grim but thankful, and brandished her sword.

"You climb. I'll kill."

We were a terror. The Nazis besieged us as we ascended those last thirty feet, but the pain of loss and the need to salvage victory proved more powerful than any necromancy. Sigrunn summoned wind and swung steel, scattering zombie parts in a gory hailstorm, while I climbed as promised, keeping my teeth bit deep into the journal. When we grabbed onto the rail of the *Logophile*, one zombie had the temerity to swing his saber at me, catching me a vicious dent across my wrist; I made sure Sigrunn had a tight grip on the rail, caught the zombie about the throat, and smashed him against the hull until his body went limp.

And then we were climbing over the side, and I felt solid wood under my feet, and looked up to see two dozen zombies engaged in battle with the animated contents of our upper holds, desperately parrying and riposting against sacks and barrels and ropes.

I grinned around the book, and made ready to do battle. But before we could raise our fists, there came a great, metallic screech from below us––and the *Little Free Library*, so burned I could see clear through its hull, shot past us at full speed, careening like a cannonball straight into the underbelly of the Nazi frigate.

The frigate's hull shattered, the runes etched there winking out like a snuffed candle. The ship lost its eldritch buoyancy and plunged out of sight, trailing embers; the *Library* fared not much better, the aft falling away to join the Nazi craft, the fore spearing up toward the stratosphere before it, too, succumbed to inertia.

Out of the smoke and chaos, gleaming in the emerald firelight, shot a familiar silver-feathered owl, which flew unerringly toward the *Logophile*'s bowsprit before transforming into a gleaming grappling hook. And behind it, trailing on the end of a retracting line, came the flying forms of Sayyida and Beth, soot-streaked and flecked with burns, but alive.

The zombies collapsed, the frigate's shifters no longer around to power them. Beth and Sayyida landed sprawling on the deck, laughing and screaming obscenities at the fallen Nazis. But then Sayyida stood with haste, elation decayed to fear at the sight of Sigrunn's wound.

"Do not say a single thing about irony," Sigrunn warned her.

Sayyida answered with a laugh, a kiss, and grateful whispers I did them the courtesy of ignoring.

"Ambrose," Beth said as she rose. "Our guests need medical assistance."

"It will be my utmost pleasure, Captain," Ambrose said, his ethereal voice vibrating the deck.

Beth stopped in front of me. "And how are you, Cragg?"

Whatever bulwark against emotion the danger afforded me was gone. It was all I could do to hand the journal to Beth and say three words.

"This is all."

"Oh, Cragg." Beth clutched the book to her chest. "I know you did all you could. Sigrunn was wounded...I..."

My hands finally free, I signed her my response. "What good are books if no people are around to enjoy them?"

She started nodding before I finished, smiling wistfully.

"I could only save one," I signed, any relief long gone. "They were all so valuable, but that one––" ––I pointed to the journal–– "––was a single person's story. I thought, we will probably find more King or Miller or M-E-L-V-I-L-L-E––"

"Yes," Beth said, nodding in comprehension. "I like to think I'd have done the same." Beth looked at the journal's covers, riffled its pages. "It's half blank—-more than half blank..." She saw the shadow on my face and held up a hand. "I actually think it's a good thing."

I raised my clay eyebrows. "What?"

She handed the journal back to me with reverence. "Once I make sure none of us bleed to death," she said, "I'll see if I can find some ink. I think..." She smiled at me. "This could be good practice."

Her implication was a starburst in my mind. I stood holding the journal, feeling the leather warming in my hands. I expected it to feel weighty, but actually, it felt quite light. It made sense; the Nazis wanted to stamp out our legend, so why not try to make it permanent?

We were a wounded crew of five, two of us unfamiliar with the paradigm running the ship. Sigrunn and Sayyida were likely to join us on the bounty rolls, and even if they didn't, we'd be pursued by the Luftwaffe as far as the biplanes' shifters would allow.

But all of that was distant birdsong in my mind; I was preparing to start our ship's log. I would write an entry for every one of our exploits here in the Broken Skies, and when the journal was full, I would seek a working press, that we might pass it on to others. Maybe I could inspire readers to see the world as we do: to value stories above riches and people above stories. Or perhaps one day time and space would heal again, and it could just be a way to pass the time.

Beth's hand could do us more justice; even Ambrose's powers could produce cleaner prose. But I was unwilling to even loosen my grip on the journal. They already had ways to make themselves heard. This time, the Book Golem would write his own book. The writing itself, regardless of anything else, was victory.

The Nazis had already burned many stories in their quest to control the world's narrative...but maybe they wouldn't burn ours.

Tyler Hayes is an anxious Muppet in a cunning writer disguise; he writes about hope, empathy, fear, people trying to move past their mistakes, and when he can, dinosaurs. His work is available from Alliteration Ink and Graveside Tales; you can find him on Twitter as @the_real_tyler.

Always A Chance

by Chelsea Counsell

EVERYTHING WAS GOING smoothly until the pirates attacked.

For thirty-six hours, Amalie and Silver had taken turns navigating the *Benbow* from Florence to Peking, trading sleep shifts so that there was always someone at the helm. Her neck itched occasionally with worry, thinking of their cargo and Grandin, the dragon trainer, who had remained below deck for the entirety of the journey. But after a breakfast of cheese and figs around sunrise, a dot appeared just above the horizon, and then she had bigger things to worry about.

Keeping her gloved hands on the steering, she leaned forward, eyeing the dot. They were passing through the Qing Empire's hinterlands. The ground below them was a speckled map of plains and ice-covered mountains. But that dot...

It was not uncommon to see other airships near industrial hubs. They'd had a near miss flying over the crowded airspace of Belgrade, and Amalie had expected the same the closer they got to Peking. But they weren't that close, and the dot kept getting bigger.

"Silver, can you make that out?" she asked.

"You see it, too?" From his long coat, Silver pulled a brass spyglass, which he held to one eye with his good hand. His other arm dropped off to nothing but a neatly pinned sleeve just above the elbow, above which sat Morpheus, a black dragon the size of a hound, its tail curled for balance around Silver's throat.

Silver hissed a breath through his teeth that made Morpheus's dark plumage ruffle. "Black flag," he said of the dot in the sky. "They're illegal freighters. It's possible that they're not pirates, just bootleggers, but at this distance, in Qing hinterland airspace, with us carrying the cargo we are? Unlikely."

Amalie clutched the helm. Her torc dragon, Ratha—a gift from her father upon graduating from the Institute—hissed and burrowed under the collar of her thick shearling coat. So much for being a guard dragon.

"What do you plan to do?" Silver asked.

"Keep going," Amalie said with a hardness in her voice that could have rent steel.

"Not 'try to lose them in the mountains'? Not 'radio for help'?"

"There will be no help out here," Amalie said, feeling irritation well inside her. Her first mission out of the Institute—a mission her father was supposed to lead, had he not disappeared—and she risked losing everything in a pirate attack. The odds had been unfairly stacked against her from the start. "We're on our own," she said. "Did you not realize that when they sent a child to do a man's job?"

"You're not a child."

Amalie's jaw tightened, and for a moment she looked only at the horizon, where Peking lay. Then she pulled a lever on the steering, releasing a hunk of meat or some other such morsel in the bowels of the ship to inspire the ship-dragon, Sparky, to light his chest fire, heat the water system, and speed up the ship—depending on how serious his cold was.

"We'll fight them if they come," she said. "I'm going to check on Grandin. Will you take the helm?"

"Of course, m'lady."

Amalie nodded and turned to duck down the ramp to the cargo hold. When she reached the hold, lit by golden lanterns on the walls, she froze as every tendon in her body locked.

In the center of the room, now free from its cage, stood a four-legged mass of sinew and muscle enameled in iridescent ivory. The mane was the most peculiar part—like blue fire quickening from crest to tail. It sent flickers of opal firelight against the walls. The dragon's skin was tessellated—dark blue ridges standing out against white shell. And two horns like crescent moons sprung from a brow over a long-whiskered snout, which puffed clouds of steam into the air.

Regardless, the strangest thing in the room was not the dragon itself but Grandin, the dragon trainer—a young woman of small, round stature with dark skin and curly hair. There was the dragon, looking like a majestic portent of death with its hand-long canines and fire-blue eyes. And there was Grandin...hugging it.

Grandin noticed Amalie and pulled back slightly, stroking a small hand down one of the dragon's haunches. Her smile was tentative.

Amalie's chest constricted painfully and her lips pulled back in a snarl. "What are you doing?" she snapped. "What did I say about letting it out of its cage?"

Grandin flinched, as if Amalie scared her more than the horse-size beast in her arms. "Tianfei doesn't like the cage," she said.

Amalie's fists balled. "You can't just give the dragon free rein of the ship because it doesn't like the cage!" she said. "There is a ship out there coming closer that is no doubt full of pirates drooling to steal that beast. Do you understand what will happen if we don't make it to Peking? Not to mention it's dangerous, just—just look at it."

Indeed, the dragon had begun to step back and forth in agitation, and the steam from its thumb-size nostrils had turned black as smoke.

"Pirates or no pirates, I have Tianfei under control," Grandin said stolidly. She patted the dragon right on the chest. "Everything will be okay. But you're making her nervous. You should go above deck for a bit, so I can calm her down."

Rage blistered on Amalie's cheeks, and deep in her coat, Ratha squirmed. How dare Grandin give her orders? That she would tell Amalie what to do on her own mission made her so angry that her mind was like mortar smashing together—she couldn't even speak. Pursing her lips, she turned and marched up the stairs, throwing the door of the hold shut behind her.

The slam shook her reverie, and she moved toward the helm a little less stormily. Silver stood there, tending the wheel. A lit pipe hung from his mouth.

"What happened?" he asked easily.

Like milk curdling in her stomach, Amalie felt a mix of anger and shame because she felt so angry. "It's my first mission and I've got some lowborn simpleton reining my dragon," she bit off. She flushed at how petulant she sounded. Her father's reputation rested on her shoulders; the peace between countries depended on getting the dragon from Florence to Peking. How could she do that if she couldn't control her own emotions?

Silver stepped away from the steering to let her regain control of the ship. With Morpheus crouched on his shoulder like a gargoyle, he moved to the banister and made himself comfortable, leaving Amalie to sulk in her thoughts at the wheel.

The dot on the northern horizon bloomed into a ship with two blade-like wings and a black-colored hull. To the east, the Great Wall snaked like a pale river through verdant trees—just beyond that was the city Peking, and though Amalie could not make out the buildings yet, she could see it in her mind's eye as she had seen it in books, with the clay tile roofs, curved eaves, and Fu Lion statues sitting at magnanimous attention.

With Sparky's help, the pace of the *Benbow* quickened, sending the landscape by more quickly. But the pirate ship—if it was a pirate ship—nonetheless managed to gain.

As it came closer, Amalie saw that the ship's wings were biplanar, tapering to points, and the hull tapered at the bow to almost a harpoon. If the *Benbow* were a harbor seal, the black ship was an orca—pointed and sharp, with a deadly bite.

For a moment, she fingered the handle of the saber at her hip. Silver reappeared from the cargo hold, and he stood tense near her, resting his hand on his cutlass.

She counted ten men on the black ship. Nine standing eagerly at its rails, and one necessarily on steering. Before she could even make out the color of their hair, she knew they were pirates, for the way they eyed her ship was nothing but predatory.

Then the black ship was upon them, and all Amalie could do was spin her hands around and around, steering in a vain attempt to circumvent them. She could almost see the bricks of the Great Wall when the black ship harpooned her bow.

It was like running aground in air. The entire *Benbow* lurched, throwing Amalie against the wheel and jarring her arms in their sockets. Silver went floundering across the planks of the deck before rolling upright and drawing his sword. Morpheus scurried up after him.

The pirates, for they were pirates, jumped from the black ship onto the deck of the *Benbow*. Three of them went for Silver, attempting to down him with their cutlasses. The rest—a half dozen—ran below decks for the cargo.

Amalie almost felt hurt that they didn't see her as a threat. Their loss.

She abandoned the helm. Caught by the black ship, the *Benbow* would keep aloft and steady so long as Sparky kept puffing. From her sheath Amalie pulled her glimmering saber, which she wielded almost as confidently as the wheel.

Silver held his own against the three pirates. They were younger and perhaps stronger than he, but Silver's sword hand was steady and quick, like a dragon bite, and Morpheus was like a second sword, slashing out with claws and teeth against the pirates' vulnerable flesh.

Amalie rushed, sword drawn, behind one of Silver's assailants, and struck the man's cutlass from his hand so that it soared over the side of the *Benbow*. As the man gaped at his empty hand, Silver used the man's shock to cut him down.

"Go!" Silver shouted to her. "The dragon!"

Amalie nodded, her heart quickening, and ran for the cargo hold, disappearing down the dark ramp. She leveled out to the sound of a wail, just as Grandin rushed the pirates, clawing at their burly arms like a wildcat.

"Get off me, girl," one of them growled, and thrust his elbow into her face, knocking her straight back to the floor.

The dragon pulled against the iron chains the pirates had swung around it, as if trying to get to Grandin's side. Dark smoke puffed from its nose.

"Alrighty, men, let's get this beast aloft," said a bald pirate with drooping earlobes. Then he noticed Amalie. They all noticed Amalie, for her sword glimmered in the dragon light.

"If you'll excuse us, miss," he said.

Amalie made no move to abandon her guard on the exit. Keeping her eyes on the pirates, she held her sword steady.

"As you like it." The bald man smiled and drew his cutlass.

Amalie backed up the ramp. She didn't want to give the man leeway, but the incline would give her the advantage, and the narrow passageway meant that she would stand between the pirates and their goal—the dragon would not leave while she still stood.

The bald man engaged her, testing her sword as she parried. He seemed to take her more seriously than the man above decks had. Maybe it was that she stood between him and his goal. Maybe it was the firelight.

She lanced out, attempting to disarm him. He parried. A quick twist of his blade and he sent his cutlass shooting toward her like a saber strike. Amalie jumped back. He struck at her more quickly, his sword biting like a cobra. She managed to parry, but only just. His sword was heavy, and though she parried his strikes, each one jarred her arms until she grew tired. With each attack, she lost ground, until she had reached where the ramp opened onto the main deck.

"Amalie!"

She turned, barely managing to parry the second blade that swooped in from behind—one of the pirates had broken away from Silver and advanced on her. The bald man saw his chance and went for her throat.

Amalie gasped as his sword—not quite parried by her own blade—pierced the thick shearling of her coat. The blade dug against her flesh, and she howled, a brutal sound that swept out of her like a whale cry.

Silver re-engaged the man who had come at her back, pulling him away, but it was too late. Amalie gripped the cut on her shoulder and felt hot blood seep through her coat.

With a hiss, Ratha scampered out from the belly of her coat and back around her neck. When the bald man swung his sword at her again, the dragon jumped across their meeting blades, scurried up the man's arm, and burrowed into his garments.

The bald man's eyes went wide and he screamed high.

Amalie stepped to the side, narrowly missing him as he danced past her, trying to get the tiny dragon out of his clothes. As he staggered, she ripped her sword through his calf, felling him to the wood floor.

"Who's next?" she started to say, but then the three pirates leading the dragon shoved past her, and she had to move back just to avoid being trampled.

The dragon shrieked like grating metal, its nostril smoke turning black as ash as it reared against the men pulling it by the heavy shackles around its limbs. But six men's brute strength was too much for it, and it was losing ground toward the side of the *Benbow*.

Fear that they would escape crashed in Amalie's chest. She threw herself at them, her sword drawn like a bolt of thunder, but one of the pirates caught his cutlass against her saber and dragged her into a fight, where she had to parry or else be cut down—she could only watch them take the dragon as she fended off his attacks.

"Let her go!" a voice shouted, and Grandin appeared from the cargo bay, her nose flushed with blood that ran down over her lips. She ran straight for the pirates, seemingly oblivious to their weapons, and lunged at one at random, biting down on a scarred bicep.

The man gave a guttural shout and yanked Grandin off him by her short, curly hair, throwing her against the deck.

Amalie's heart lodged in her throat as she thrust her sword first one way, then another, trying to shake off the man who had engaged her. The dragon's frantic blue mane danced against her eyes, and Amalie knew she was only moments from losing everything—from irredeemably failing her father, the Institute, and herself.

The pirates threw a steel lasso around the dragon's neck, tightening it like a noose as they dragged it toward their ship.

On the deck, forgotten, Grandin crawled to her knees and raised her fingers, blowing a sharp, high-pitched whistle that broke over the noise of the fighting.

At once, the dragon's entire demeanor changed. If Amalie had thought it dangerous before, she had no idea what to think of it now, for it made the creature Grandin had hugged in the cargo bay look like a birth-wet kitten.

With a roar like an engine seizing, the dragon swept its muscular tail like an undertow at the knees of the men surrounding it, knocking them to the ground. The blue-white flames of its mane grew almost too bright to look at. Then it opened its mouth wide like the inhale of a bellows and fire erupted the deck, blue and liquid as lava.

Amalie jumped back toward the steering, scared for her own skin, as grown men screamed wet, guttural screams. The air grew sharp with the stench of blackened wood and charred flesh. Not all of the pirates had been burned—but the ones who hadn't jumped over the side of the *Benbow* onto the black ship, retreating, and dragged their burned counterparts with them.

Amalie stood in shock, clutching a rail, as the black ship pulled away from the *Benbow*. Grandin clutched Tianfei with tears running down her cheeks. Amalie felt a pull of sorrow and shame in her chest, seeing her cry. Then a downward lurch awakened her to her senses—Sparky was not lit. They were falling.

"Get ready to come down hard!" she shouted, running to the steering. She took hold and hooked her feet under the crossbar. She pulled the lever that would feed Sparky, hoping that the many, many apparatuses that could fail would not.

The *Benbow* plunged toward the ground, which had cropped up in tidy squares of pavilions and terraces, flying by too quickly and too close.

Amalie looked across the burning deck to where Grandin held on to the dragon, which clung to the wood of the deck by its claws. Silver and Morpheus were on the other side of the flames, holding tight to a guardrail.

Amalie pushed another lever, pitching the ship forward. The wings needed to catch the wind—they had to. Her heart hammered in her chest, knowing the ground was coming closer and closer to their hull. There was always the chance that the ship-dragon wouldn't light properly. Always a chance.

And then she felt it, a lurch forward like the kick of an engine, and she pulled the lever to even them out as Sparky lit.

AMALIE STOOD IN A COURTYARD just inside the Qing palace, waiting for the Qing ambassador to give them the exit documents for the mission.

Silver was there, too, with lit pipe, watching Morpheus stalk blood-red koi at the edge of a pond. The *Benbow* had been damaged in the fight and the resulting rough landing, so he waited to hear whether they could repair it before they returned to Florence.

Amalie strode nearer to where Grandin stood, speaking with the Qing dragon trainer—a black-haired woman in a pale green dress, who gave an enthusiastic "mmm" to everything Grandin said about the dragon.

Amalie watched Grandin speak about the dragon—how her hands moved as she spoke, she was so passionate, and how the dragon would nuzzle her shoulders with its snout whenever it wasn't getting enough attention from her. Amalie tried to reconcile this gentle creature with the terror she had seen on the ship. Were they really the same?

When the Qing trainer left to get the ambassador, Amalie approached Grandin, who was stroking the dragon's snout—probably saying goodbye.

For a moment, Amalie was silent, watching, feeling something like an intruder on their intimate moment. But then she cleared her throat, and Grandin turned.

"Grandin, I wanted to say how sorry I am for the way I acted," Amalie said. "I shouldn't have yelled at you. I didn't understand...but I should have trusted your expertise."

She tensed, expecting Grandin to bite in the same way she'd expected the dragon to.

"That's all right," Grandin said. "You were just scared."

Amalie nodded, impressed again with her ease. "I hope that when we go back to Florence, I can explain to the Institute what a help you've been."

Grandin started. "I'm not going back to Florence," she said.

Amalie thought for sure she had misheard her. "What?"

"I'm staying here. Wherever Tianfei goes, that's where I'm needed."

Amalie felt herself deflate slightly. "Oh. Oh, I had no idea." She couldn't imagine giving up Florence, her home, for a dragon. The bond between them must be even greater than she understood. "Well. Perhaps I'll have another mission in Peking sometime. We could see each other again."

"I would like that," Grandin said. Then she smiled, in a way a mischievous cherub might, and gestured toward Tianfei's long-whiskered, ivory snout. "Do you want to pet her?" she asked.

With a smile, Amalie stepped forward and allowed herself to be guided toward new experience.

"ALWAYS A CHANCE" © 2018 by Chelsea Counsell

Chelsea Counsell is an aspiring tea master and expert dog petter. She lives in Massachusetts, where she writes about telekinesis and the oppression of women. She is an alumna of Viable Paradise XX and Futurescapes 2018. On Twitter she's @ChelseaCounsell and her website is www.chelseacounsell.com.

What A Tea Witch Promises

by C. C. S. Ryan

JENOYE PADDED THROUGH the quiet corridors of the leisure airship *Starlight Spectacle*. It was her fourth day on the ship. She had made it to the semifinal round of the competition to be the *Spectacle*'s first resident tea witch, and she had things to do before everyone else woke up.

As she approached the topmost observation deck, over which the ship's silvery, almost entirely ornamental sail soared toward the fading stars, she narrowed her eyes. Someone was up on the mast, in the ropes, well past the reach of the muted lights on the deck. Jenoye had never gotten around to taking an airship cruise before, so maybe, she thought, that was normal.

Jenoye removed a roll of silk from her robes and pulled vials and bundles out of the many pockets of her apron. She spread the cloth on the deck and arranged her ingredients on it. The eight items she'd chosen would become more potent when they were touched by the first rays of the sun. None of the other competitors were in sight, but she supposed they each had their own ways of preparing. She sat back and waited for the sun to crest the vast horizon. A good time to meditate, maybe. Just cast back the stiff hood of her formal cloak, open her witch-eye and—

The pain almost made her fall over. Distress, sharp and deep, came from the figure above her. Jenoye got to her feet and stared upwards as all three of her eyes filled with tears. Blinking them away, she tongued a bit of foxfire moss from a pocket and gently blew a puff of light from her mouth. She sent it spiraling up the mast.

"Good morning. Are you all right?" Jenoye asked gently. The witch-light carried her voice and sight up with it. She could just make out a face—vaguely familiar, maybe featured on one of the posters promoting the airship's attractions: a magical ice rink, a banquet hall with a starry sky, the tea witch competition, a pirate show... Yes, that was it. An actor.

"What? Who—oh. One of the tea witches. I'm all right. How...?"

"May I speak with you?"

"I..."

In the witch-light, Jenoye could just make out the rope that was loosely wrapped around the woman's hand. She didn't know what she would do if the actor's anguish caused her to...to do something rash.

The sharp pounding of the actor's heart layered on top of Jenoye's anxious pulse. She closed her witch-ears. "You're not Endoan, right? Has a tea witch ever given you a service? If you come down, it would be my pleasure to offer you one. It—it may suggest some solution to your dilemma. Please? At the very least, it should taste good!" A bit undignified, but Jenoye hoped she'd covered her terror and sounded friendly and professional.

The woman sighed, tightened the rope, and slid-scrambled toward the deck. Jenoye felt a rush of relief, and closed her witch-eye tight—it was rude to open witch-senses around others without permission.

The actor approached Jenoye, keeping plenty of space between them, and looked her up and down. "I don't know that tea can help, uh..."

Jenoye cleared her throat. "I'm Jenoye. It's not simply tea—although it's good tea! It's genuine magic. Sure, tea witches can't fly like wizards, but we have other talents, including the powers of insight." She touched her closed eyelid and her ears, and was gratified when the other woman looked curious. "And you are?"

"Lieute—Andev, just Andev. I'm a...performer. I didn't think tea witches were quite real," Andev said. Her eyes drifted toward the graying sky. "But my problems aren't something I can chat about with a stranger."

Jenoye didn't need her witch-senses to see the hollows in Andev's cheeks or the harsh dark circles under her eyes, interrupting the soft brown of her face. Jenoye was surprised, though, to see tangled scars that trailed across Andev's tight jaw and disappeared under a high collar. Maybe acting was a rougher trade than she knew.

Jenoye nodded. "Well, sometimes the client doesn't have to tell me anything. Did you see the first round? That gentleman hardly had to speak at all."

Andev cocked her head. "I caught a little of it, and the second round yesterday. I didn't quite understand what was happening. Although they did seem happy afterwards, your clients."

"Well, a tea witch helps a client address something in their heart, slight or profound. These ingredients here are mostly simple herbs and dried tea leaves, right? That's where we start. We blend them with magic, and we conjure sweet fancies—they may look like bonbons, but they also do a share of the work. That's how we reach a person's heart, to restore balance or name a hidden fear or rediscover joy." And then she was supposed to carry a bit of it with her, but for the past two days, Jenoye had been so focused on the competition that she'd only brought back tiny shards of openness and joy from those clients.

"But is it always so...public?"

"Oh, no! Only for competitions. If you ask for a private tea service, I'm bound to help and to never tell anyone what happened. That's the promise. If I broke it, I wouldn't be a tea witch anymore."

Andev gave Jenoye a hard stare, and she had to fight the urge to step back. Behind Andev, the golden edge of the sun spilled across the horizon.

Finally, Andev nodded. "I think you're telling the truth. Offering me a lifeline. But why? You don't know me, and I have no money. I have nothing."

Wisps of glowing sparks rose from the ingredients at their feet. Jenoye bent to gather them up and waved off Andev's hesitant gesture of assistance. "Rules are rules. A tea witch is obligated to help someone in distress. Just like how Endoans always offer a cup of tea—the regular kind, I mean—to anyone who asks."

Andev shook her head. "Endoa. So strange. All right, I'll try your tea service."

"This way," said Jenoye. "We can do it before the competition begins."

Andev followed her. "It's important to you, this competition."

Jenoye hugged her bundle to her chest. "It's everything. After I graduated, I was itinerant. I like meeting new people. But for some, if you don't have your own appointed position or your own shop..." She reminded herself that she was a professional, and hastily straightened and tucked the bundle under her arm. "So, tell me about your show!"

Andev was silent and Jenoye had to glance back to see if she was still there. Then she shrugged and pointed at a poster on the wall ahead of them. "Can't say much more than that." Andev couldn't seem to actually look at the poster herself.

Two fine portraits depicted Andev and a woman whose face was partly hidden by a cockaded captain's hat. Both wore uniforms that were surely sharper than any real pirate had ever worn. Beneath the portraits, multi-hued and gold-tinted calligraphy declared:

The days of piracy are long over in the skies of Endoa, but everyone loves a swashbuckler! For your delight, before the final round of the tea witchery competition, you may experience the thrill and frisson of a piratical boarding!

Duels and derring-do? Yes! Risk to yourselves or your heirlooms? No!

Don't miss this event in the banquet hall with our handsome band of privateers, led by Captain Toural and First Lieutenant Andev!

"I...see. Well, this way."

JENOYE SAT FACING ANDEV at her cabin table. Tight quarters meant that scents would be more potent, for better or for worse, and she would need to be mindful.

With Andev's permission, Jenoye took her hands and recited the invocation and pledge for a private service. She opened her witch-eye, and her second pair of ears twitched out ever so slightly. A quiet moment passed while she set out three small pots and filled them with spring water from the mountains back home. Another bit of foxfire- moss and a whisper against each pot set a softly- colored flame around its base.

The first pot was to open the heart. Sometimes that was enough. The second pot, if needed, was to touch the heart, and the third pot was to change the heart. Jenoye had only used a third pot twice in her career so far. But she didn't know how well any of it would work on a foreigner.

"How...how much can you see?" whispered Andev.

"Not specifics, usually," Jenoye said. "And it's all confidential."

Andev's panic had resurfaced and wasn't subsiding. How could Jenoye get this foreigner to trust her?

Some of the fear and pain in Andev's heart flowed from the distant west. Between that and the way she spoke, Jenoye had a guess as to where she was from. What was it Jenoye had heard about people from there? They swore on blood, didn't they?

Before she could second-guess herself, Jenoye pushed back her hood and took out the tiny, sharp blade that she used for ingredients like citrus peels. A light prick of her finger, and a drop of blood welled out. "I promise you my secrecy," she said.

Andev's fear eased a little. But now what to do with this drop of blood?

She'd have to keep improvising. Jenoye put an orange leaf on a tray and let the blood fall onto it. Then she carefully released a drop of shimmering, hot water from the first pot onto it. Both liquids disappeared into a tiny scarlet puff.

Jenoye doubted that was what Westerners did. Still, it seemed good enough for Andev, who made a nod of satisfaction and held out her finger. Jenoye hadn't expected that, but now she had to go with it. She swallowed and repeated the steps.

Time to begin the actual tea.

The first little cup was stoneware, rough and thick, like a child might use. The scents that rose from the tea came from as many Western fruits and spices as Jenoye could find in her collection. Scent was a direct route to a client's past. She took the first sip and passed it to Andev.

Andev breathed in deeply—just what she was supposed to do—and then tossed it back in one gulp. Definitely not what she was supposed to do. But her eyes unfocused slightly, and after a moment, she spoke. "When I was little, before...before things changed, if something scared me, I'd make a point of doing it anyway. But now, I'm afraid of...the performance." She shook her head. "I don't have the words." She stared into the empty cup.

Jenoye waited for three breaths, then drew a second, stronger cup from the pot. She took her sip and passed it to Andev. "Not stage fright?"

"No." Andev swallowed the tea and closed her eyes. "Have you ever experienced something you couldn't help but see over and over, where even thinking about it made you sick?"

Jenoye knew of it: the injury to the heart that reopened itself. One of her teachers had decided to study tea witchery because of how tea services had stopped her from waking sobbing in the night. Jenoye conjured a small sphere of warm apple and molasses, and passed the fancy on a tiny tray to Andev.

"Never knew you could use magic to make sweets." Andev hesitantly tasted it, then ate it all. "It's so warm." She put a hand on her chest.

The obvious problem was that Andev needed assistance in overcoming her hurt so that she could perform. But there was something else. The warmth of the sweet wasn't going to get Jenoye there, but at least it would make Andev feel a little better. Her witch-gaze roamed over Andev and settled on the recent past, trailing above her like an angry storm.

Jenoye took the cup back and looked at the traces. Some of the leaves were twisted in on themselves. Jenoye rolled them between her fingers. Andev, she thought, was not an actor.

On to the next course, then. Jenoye wrapped the second teapot in gentle spring rainclouds. The tea that she steeped now smelled of safety: toasted grains, warm cotton, the fur of a cat lazing by a fire. She warmed the cup with witch-fire before pouring. After her sip, she placed the cup and a tray with a silvery, sugar-frosted berry into Andev's hands. Jenoye had never seen the fruit before; she had conjured it from Andev's heart.

Andev took a sip of tea and nibbled the berry. "I was picking frostberries when they took me," she said, so quietly that

Jenoye could hardly hear. Tears spilled down her cheeks, into her cup. Jenoye felt Andev's heart crack open.

"You don't have to say anything," Jenoye said quickly.

Andev shook her head. "I need to now," she whispered roughly. "I—I don't ever want to hold a sword again, even a toy sword. I got away! And I thought I was free, but Toural, first mate on the ship I escaped—I might've set fire to it, a bit—she's off raising havoc on her own now. It's all she knows how how to do. And she tracked me down for this scheme. I was..." Andev flushed. She stared at her feet for a moment, then let out a short bark of bitter laughter. "She used to call me her protégé, the one she'd been able to whip into exactly what she wanted. I'm the linchpin of this plan. She's had me training these poor actors. They don't know anything. I haven't been able to tell anyone! I—I'm a fugitive. If Toural turns me in, I won't see the sky again for ten years, not till execution day. And so I can only do what Toural tells me to do. I'm useless. A coward."

Jenoye pulled threads of insight from Andev's heart and stitched them together. Andev was a real pirate. Well, not exactly—as a young woman, really barely more than a child, she'd been pressed into a pirate crew. Just as rumors claimed could happen in the West. But she had managed to free herself. Not right away, not before maelstroms of blood and terror. Those memories were the wounds in her heart. Now Toural had essentially run a sword through Andev and twisted the blade.

Jenoye tried to keep the shock from her face while she conjured another fancy, this one a candied hazelnut, flecked with gold and wrapped in a cloud of autumn sweetgrass. She took a deep breath and put it directly into Andev's hands. "No, Andev. You've been so brave."

Andev ate it slowly, as though afraid of being overpowered by the flavor. "Have I?" She wiped at her face with a flaxen napkin. Her heart lightened and then sank again. "It doesn't change anything. When the 'performance' begins, Toural will have the troupe gather everyone's valuables. She'll set off a flare, and a skycab she's stolen will come for her, or us." She made as though to spit, but stopped herself. "No security on this ship! I didn't believe it'd be so, but you Endoans... You can't stop her."

Jenoye poured more tea into Andev's tear-stained cup, to ease her worry. "Oh, yes we can," Jenoye said. She had a plan. "Just come watch the competition. Bring Toural."

Andev, clearly puzzled but also less tightly coiled than before, watched as Jenoye conducted the end of the service. "I believe you, but I don't know why."

"Then I'll see you there," Jenoye said.

Andev left. Jenoye gripped the edge of the table for a moment, pushing down a surge of nausea. She loved a challenge that played to her strengths, and she had promised to help, but had she made the right decision?

Jenoye shook her head and reorganized her ingredients. She had work to do, and midmorning was on its way.

JENOYE HARDLY NOTICED the bright blue of the sky or heard the drums and applause as she climbed to the competition platform. Was Andev there? She was, and so was Toural, smirking faintly. The other troupe members jostled behind them. Jenoye opened her witch-eye just a sliver and cast it over

Toural. It was a tea witch competition, after all; no one could expect to be entirely shielded from witch-senses here.

Despite Toural's sturdy exterior, she was shrouded in chaotic feelings. Not the thunderheads of greed and bloodlust that Jenoye might have expected from a pirate (though there was certainly some of that) but a persistent haze of resentment and bitterness.

Jenoye was third, and she wasn't sure that she would survive the wait. She made herself focus on developing and rehearsing her strategies. The first two witches did well; though Jenoye wasn't watching them, she felt the bright hearts of their clients as they stepped down.

Finally, she was called. Jenoye arranged her ingredients and utensils on the table, working to look calm.

The host called for clients. It was time.

Jenoye pointed into the crowd of sunlit faces and waving hands. In the loudest voice she could manage, she called out, "Captain Toural!"

Toural took a step back. Andev glanced up at Jenoye, questioning, and then Jenoye's witch-ears heard her say to Toural, "Go on, it's harmless." The rest of the troupe took up the cause, cheering for Toural, and soon enough, Toural put on a smile and took her seat.

Jenoye began the competition invocation and set out her teapots. Her hands were shaking as she chose her first ingredients. Toural would volunteer nothing, not like Andev had. And yet Jenoye's choices still had to be perfect. Her flavors had to be so enticing, so close to Toural's heart, that she would never think of leaving the stage.

For the entire first pot, neither of them uttered a word, but Jenoye strained to open her eyes and ears as widely as she could. Toural had her own wounds, but she also had thick scar tissue that prevented Jenoye from reaching her. Finally, at the end of the first pot, heavy with the nostalgia-inducing herbs from the West that had unlocked Andev's memories, Jenoye began to find her way in. Like Andev, everything had been taken from Toural. But Toural believed that she took only what she was owed, and over the years, this unreasoned belief, fed by greed, had only taken stronger root in her heart.

Toural was alarmed now, but Jenoye had made the heart-touch successfully. They were connected, however much Toural was fighting it. Jenoye searched for sources of joy and empathy in Toural's tangle of thoughts and memories.

The first fancy of the second pot was faceted like a gem, with the same green luster as the stones in Toural's ears and belt. It shattered between her teeth, releasing the sweet rush of victory inside. Jenoye watched Toural carefully, looking for the light of remembered triumph in her eyes.

When Toural's jaw lifted, Jenoye poured tea into a little cup that was decorated with gold vines on the outside, but rough and unfinished inside. She wafted the scented steam toward Toural, who reflexively breathed in as she took the cup. This tea was as down-to-earth as the fancy had been heady, made with leaves from a deep valley, the humblest of toasted barley, and the clearest of snowmelt. This was to ground Toural in the present.

Jenoye spoke silently, directly to Toural's heart, weaving thin strands of joy and clarity into images and meaning for her alone. "The passengers on this ship are not your Western tyrants, warlords, and aristocrats, Toural. They've taken nothing from you, neither gold nor blood. Their boots aren't the ones that have been on your neck." Another fancy, and another tiny cup. "They're ordinary people, like you. Their losses will hurt them."

Jenoye suppressed a flinch at the spiky paths of Toural's heart. Thick, scarred briars twisted toward the west, marked by heartbreak and loss. To be sure, Toural hadn't been forced down her road. She'd made many terrible choices over the years and had rarely resisted her darker impulses. But her memories of oppression and brutality, which seeded her resentment, were also genuine.

The third pot.

Jenoye spoke aloud, softly enough that only Toural could hear. "This third pot is to change the heart. But not for me to change you. It's for you to change yourself. I'm only here to open a way."

She felt Toural's heart shudder, but the captain didn't move.

This pot was black, cast iron with a pattern of waves and birds that held the viewer's eye. Jenoye silently asked for the grace of her mentors' mentors to make her blend potent. On an impulse, she slipped in the orange leaf from earlier.

This tea changed significantly as it brewed. First, she poured a smoky cup accompanied by a lozenge of layered memories that made Toural dwell anew within her own sense of loss, to remember how it felt when it was fresh. Secondly, a sharp cup, to which Jenoye added directly a handful of fancies composed of small silver pearls. They tasted of metal and tears.

Toural reached for the cup with shaking hands, as though daring herself to complete the ceremony. As each pearl burst in Toural's mouth, she was flooded with the full strength of the pain and fear a passenger would feel as they lost their heirlooms to her.

Toural's face became ashen as she swallowed the final mouthful. Her eyes were fixed on the iron pot. The connection between them choked as though Toural had caught it in her fist.

Cold sweat ran down Jenoye's spine and all three of her eyes ached. She glanced around for the first time since the service had begun. A heavy silence hung over the crowd, and the judges stared down at her.

Andev, eyebrows knitted together, caught her gaze. "What are you doing?" Andev mouthed. But it was time for the final cup of this final pot, the real test of Jenoye's skills. The connection was still there. She needed to use it while she still could.

Jenoye had thought to give Toural a taste of peace and strength here, a glimpse of what could be hers if only she didn't carry out her plan. She listened more carefully to the thorns holding back Toural's quaking heart.

The last cup was tiny but profoundly bitter. The fancy that Jenoye gave Toural was both the most astringent and the sweetest she had ever made. She had taken a risk and made it from scratch that morning, out of real sugar and citron, but now she would change the magic that it would carry. Jenoye breathed on it and conjured a ray of sunlight, a soft taste of sky, and the freedom of the wind to accompany it into Toural's mouth. She wrapped the teacup in piercing starlight.

"Be free of all this," Jenoye whispered, and she felt Toural's heart clench.

Toural swallowed the fancy, drank down the tea, and began to sob. Not helpless tears like Andev had wept, but a wretched howl. The thicket around her heart tore itself apart. She swept her arm across the table and Jenoye tried not to flinch as her best cups and trays shattered on the stage. Toural buried her face in her hands, and then she stood, knocking over her chair.

"What's left of me now, then? What else do I know to do? What is to fill my life if not some small measure of payback? If I have to feel their pain and my own—you may as well have murdered me," Toural said raggedly, and she stalked off the stage.

"You'll find a new heading," Jenoye said. Toural was already out of earshot, but maybe Jenoye's words would reach her anyway.

The judges spoke in strained, rapid whispers. Jenoye sat, frozen. It was done. She ought to feel either pride in her work or regret at her recklessness, probably, but instead she felt dizzy, as though she had just looked down before the last step on a rope bridge.

In the distance, a scarlet flare rose into the sky, calling Toural's skycab, but only Jenoye and Andev saw it.

Jenoye tried to breathe evenly. She quickly recited the closure and knelt to gather the shards of her things. The host rushed to announce an intermission and the muttering crowd dissolved.

Andev crouched next to Jenoye, and this time, Jenoye let her help. "I could probably fix this," Andev suggested, holding up two halves of a cup.

Jenoye forced a smile and felt it go askew on her lips. "Don't know if I'll be needing it anytime soon."

"What? You were incredible. I—"

"You've got a job to do." Jenoye took out a stoppered bottle from a hip pocket. "Here. A tea to steady you through the performance. You and the troupe need to get paid. Go on, you'd better help them get ready." She pressed the bottle on Andev and hurried away to her cabin.

JENOYE SORTED THROUGH her damaged tools in a daze. She hadn't entirely thought through the consequences of success. Now, when she tried, her mind just turned away.

When she was done salvaging what she could, it was nearly performance time. She might as well go and see if her tea had worked. Right? No one would recognize her in regular clothes with her hair curled over her witch-eye and ears. She took her cloak off and finally felt something: a strange sense of relief. For the first time in weeks, she wasn't fretting about the competition.

The first thing Jenoye saw in the banquet hall was a board with the names of the two finalists. Her name wasn't there. It hurt, but not as much as she'd expected it to.

Half of the troupe was present, dressed as archaic naval officers and mingling. Dancing had just begun when the faux pirates burst in, led by Andev in the captain's hat. Andev stood tall and delivered her lines boldly, and then there was a great deal of acrobatic fencing and dramatic fisticuffs between the "pirates" and the "officers."

Finally, with most of the pirates vanquished, Andev approached Jenoye, followed by a spotlight. In one hand, she gripped a rope that dropped from the ceiling, and in the other, a camellia.

Bemused, Jenoye felt Andev silently ask for her permission. Jenoye's witch-ears weren't open, but it seemed they still had some connection. Not sure what she was agreeing to, she nodded.

Andev placed the flower in Jenoye's lapel, swept an arm around her, wrapped the rope around them both, shouted some ridiculous, defiant lines to the crowd, and then—

Jenoye's feet left the ground. "What—!" She gasped as they flew up toward the starry ceiling. They soared out of the light to a shadowed balcony where the troupe's waiting hands helped them land. Jenoye could barely hear the pleased roar of the crowd over the pounding of her own pulse.

Andev released Jenoye and stood back. She rubbed the back of her neck. "I do beg your pardon,; I know that was very silly. Toural hadn't written an ending, y'see. I had to do something. Now I hope I'm done with all of this forever." She returned the mostly empty bottle of nerve-steadying tea to Jenoye, and then Andev's face grew serious. "But...your chance to be the tea witch of the *Starlight Spectacle*. Is it gone?"

Jenoye tried to summon her professional face, but Andev seemed to read the answer anyway. "Oh. No, no! I didn't—I'll go tell the judges. I'll tell them everything. Surely they'll—"

"It's all right," Jenoye said. And it was, but why? She uncorked the bottle and shook out the last few drops into her mouth. "I—I did what a tea witch promises. If I hadn't helped you, I wouldn't be a tea witch. And honestly? A tea witch is all I've ever wanted to be."

"WHAT A TEA WITCH PROMISES" © 2018 by C.C.S. Ryan

C. C. S. Ryan is a class IV corporeal free-roaming apparition. If you ask her if she is a god, she will say yes. She likes stories in which genres mingle and the girl gets the girl. Her writing has appeared in Fireside and Farstrider. Find her at ccsryan.com or @wintersweet on Twitter.

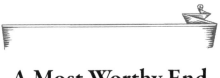

A Most Worthy End

by Timothy Shea

THE ENDS DON'T JUSTIFY the means.

A short, simple turn of phrase, one that has served as a cornerstone of moral philosophy for pretty much as long as moral philosophizing has been a thing. Plato said it. Aquinas said it. Even thinkers with ostensibly nothing else in common—Ayn Rand and Noam Chomsky, for instance—had jumped on the anti-Consequentialist bandwagon at some point in their lives. The message those six words embody is the touchstone of mental juggernauts, tirelessly explored and expounded upon and explored again by some of the greatest minds humanity has ever known.

And, to Abrams Miller, it was complete bunk.

Now, it wasn't as if he suffered from a total lack of empathy, or that he held no appreciation of what it meant to follow a higher calling. He cared about other people. At least he thought he did. And he respected those that walked the path of righteousness for righteousness's sake, even if he didn't follow them. Blessed be the names of Plato and Aristotle and all that. Theirs was a noble calling, truly. It just wasn't for him.

No, as far as his own life was concerned, Abrams preferred a more Machiavellian approach. It was better to be successful than to be righteous. After all, Socrates had wound up sucking hemlock while the Athenian elders went on to die peacefully in their beds. So what if his name had lived on through the ages while those same elders had melted quickly into obscurity? That knowledge could hardly offer succor to a corpse.

And as for the others, the Thomas Aquinas-types who had pinned their moral certitude on a belief in their God, Abrams felt nothing but utter contempt. Theirs were nothing but lives wasted on a lie.

How could he be so sure of himself? How could he be so certain in his condemnation of other's certainty? It was simple, really.

When those men had lived, beating their chests and preaching their faith in the divine, God—the real one—hadn't even been born yet.

"DAD, I'M COLD," AIZIKA muttered, miserable as a knife-like breeze cut through the dark ringlets of her hair.

Abrams didn't answer at first. He let his gaze continue to wander across the Behemoth's open-air deck, taking everything in with the cold precision of a dispassionate fanatic; Captain Samson perched on the steering platform, the seedy-looking crew milling between cargo pallets, his own two portos and muledroid tucked safely away on the meager square of planking that his coin had purchased. Shrouding it all was the persistent, impermeable shadow of the vessel's helium bladder.

"Dad," Aizika whined again.

"Shh," Abrams chided as he looked down at his young daughter. Her face was turned up towards him, cherry-red cheeks shining out from the inadequate protection of her over-sized hood. "These are bad men, girl, and they have better things to do than listen to a ten-year-old's cries. If they hear you, they might just cut out your tongue."

"I can still cry without a tongue," she shrewdly pointed out. "I just wouldn't be able to talk."

"Then you won't like what they cut next," he warned her. Sometimes the girl's precociousness still took him off- guard. And worried him. If she had any idea of why they were making the Pilgrimage...

"Why do we have to take a skyship?" she asked. She still sounded unhappy, but her question was noticeably hushed. "Why can't we sail on the water like we did before? It was never this cold down there."

"Because," he answered, "you can't get to God from the ocean."

"Why not?"

"You'll see, girl. You'll see."

Taking a deep breath, Abrams stared forward along their path. The glaring light cascading down past the helium bladder was deceptive. In the distance, barely visible, the steel blue of the ocean met with the unrepentant darkness of a storm system. Their crossing of the Pacific would be neither peaceful nor pleasant.

The sight of the gathering clouds was enough to make him queasy with dread. And, for one brief moment of weakness, he longed for the days of his youth when the journey could be made in hours instead of weeks. What was it his mother had called them? Bow-wings and air busses? He looked back fondly on the memory, his legs dangling from a padded chair, a nice man bringing him peanuts and pop. How long had it been since he'd had a peanut?

As quickly as the thought came to him, he shook it away as the blasphemy it was. He couldn't claim understanding of God's Revolution. He didn't know why the old world had to be destroyed in favor of the new, but he knew it was good. No nations, no wars, no pollution. And soon, if he just kept his faith, he would be elevated to greatness. God had spoken to him.

That didn't make the coming storm any less daunting. But it was necessary, the first of many sacrifices demanded by humanity's only true higher power.

THE STORM LASTED THREE days. Three days of rain, three days of darkness, three days of stomach-churning agony as the three-hundred-meter Behemoth was tossed through the skies like a dead leaf in an autumn gale. The engines screamed and the wind howled until the two noises merged into the incessant shriek of a nightmare's orchestra. Aizika endured all of it in a petrified silence.

Her stomach heaved over and over again during those three days, and between each spasming wretch, she wondered over and over again why they were there; why her father insisted on suffering through a Pilgrimage. She told her herself that it was for her, that he was doing it to buy her a better life, but she knew it was a lie. The man never did anything if it wasn't for himself. He hadn't even been willing to move back to Washington City when Mother had gotten sick.

She shivered constantly as the days dragged on, the worn fabric of Mother's rain-soaked sweatshirt plastered to her skin. The last trace of the woman's scent had been swallowed by the storm. All Aizika could smell was the static-tinged downpour cut by the sweat and terror of the crew. All she could hear were their shouted curses as they trimmed flaps and adjusted ballast and fought desperately to keep the skyship upright. She'd watched as two of the men were dragged over the guardrails by the storm, their screams quickly lost as they plummeted to a fate far below.

Their deaths went un-mourned. The surviving crewmen scarcely had time to eat, let alone to commemorate their fallen comrades. Aizika clutched desperately to the unadorned, utilitarian bulk of the four-legged muledroid, praying to God for the storm to pass. Her father crouched alone on the opposite side of the deck. The Behemoth continued to sway, and the rain continued to lash. Aizika felt she was trapped inside a hellish eternity.

And then, eventually, eternity passed. The skies cleared into a star-strewn black as the air quieted into an eerie chill. Aizika relinquished her grip on the muledroid and tried to stand, stumbling off- balance when the deck failed to shift beneath her feet. Her father was standing by one of the guard rails, peering at something below.

"Here, girl," he called softly to her.

Aizika hesitated. The illusion of safety created by the guardrails had been shattered by the storm, and her feet refused to carry her anywhere near the edge of the deck. But her father beckoned her again, and slowly, she moved to comply. The rhythmic squelch of her footfalls seemed to clash irreverently with the loud snoring of the Behemoth's exhausted crew. Coming within a few feet of the rail, she paused again.

"Come look," he told her, a crooked finger pointing down over the side.

Wary, she watched him for a moment, but saw no sign of the manic detachment that seemed to grip him at times. All she saw on his face was...awe. Her curiosity overcame her fear and she walked the final three steps to the edge.

Leaning carefully over the guardrail, Aizika had expected to be met with the inky black of the ocean. Instead she was greeted by a milky gray extending as far as she could see. A gasp left her lips. The moon, just cresting the horizon, sent a brilliant sliver of light across the mysterious world below. She stared in silence for a long while, sharing in her father's mesmerized stupor.

"Is that...ice?" she asked eventually. Her eyes were adjusting now. Shadows marring the brilliant facade became towering peaks or deep crevices that looked impassible to anything made for land or sea.

"Yes," her father said. "The Hau Freeze."

"How...how did this happen?"

"We don't know. It's a mystery. A miracle, really. God saw fit its creation, and the angels made it so."

Aizika watched the endless shield of ice drift below them, trying to find some meaning in the jagged shards reaching up into the night sky. It stared back, an enigmatic canvas, cold and menacing.

"Why?" was all she could bring herself to say.

"Because God willed it," her father answered. "To protect herself from those who would see the New Kingdom destroyed. And to keep away those who aren't worthy."

"And we're worthy?" she asked.

"Yes," he answered, sounding torn between confidence and apprehension. "I've been summoned in my dreams."

Aizika didn't know what to say to that. She turned her attention back to the Freeze, and her father placed a hand on her shoulder. She shivered.

His touch held neither warmth nor comfort.

ABRAMS SEETHED, BUT kept his face neutral. He hoped he was misreading the situation, but knew he wasn't. Up on the steering platform, Captain Samson was engaged in a hushed but animated conversation with his first mate, both of their gazes flickering frequently towards the horizon. The rest of the crew was likewise arrayed at the front of the Behemoth, staring ahead. All of them were restless. All of them were riveted by what lay beyond, turning back only to cast brief, malicious glares towards Abrams.

The cause of the sailors' apprehension was obvious. Dominating the horizon, and growing larger by the minute, the dark, brooding mass of the Island towered. It had looked benign enough when they'd first spotted land, two dark smears rising up from the endless sheets of ice. The slope of the twin mountains had appeared so gentle that they looked little more than glorified hills.

Now, an hour's journey had laid bare the mountains' deception. The skyship's altimeter read 2,500 meters, and though they were still several kilometers from where they broached the ice, both mountains clearly swelled to peaks high overhead. The sheer power of the landscape made Abrams feel like they were nearing the edge of the world. It was, he thought, a home worthy of a god.

"Mr. Miller," the captain summoned him, his voice harsh and uncompromising.

So that was it then. Abrams suppressed a grimace and made his way over to the captain's platform. "Yes?" he asked. It was a struggle to keep hostility from the simple question, but, biting his cheek, he managed.

"A situation has come up that necessitates a change to our agreement," the captain began stiffly. "We'll no longer be able to traverse up to the 4,200 meters required to deposit you at the summit. Instead, we will maintain our present altitude. My first mate informs me there is a path on the southern slope of the mountain. You and your equipment will disembark there."

"A situation," Abrams repeated, letting a biting dose of sarcasm slip into the words. "By which you of course you mean that your crew refuses to comply with our agreement. Shocking."

"If you're dissatisfied with our service," the other man countered drily, "perhaps next time you should hire a courier service to provide you transport."

"I hired you and your crew," Abrams replied, scowling, "precisely because you told me you would go where courier services wouldn't. And, I'll remind you, I paid a premium for this.

You were supposed to be tough. Fearless! Clearly, those qualities fall considerably short of what was advertised."

"Watch yourself, Mr. Miller," Captain Samson warned.

"Or what?" Abrams hissed before he could be stopped by his better judgement.

"Or you'll find I'll alter our agreement further," he answered, cryptic and menacing. "I assure you, the new terms will be even less to your liking. You're leaving my ship with your lives and freedom intact. There are not many that can make that claim. Consider yourself lucky."

Luck was the last thing Abrams felt, but he recognized a losing battle when faced with one. It was just a test. Another test to be passed, and when he'd earned God's favor, he'd have his revenge on these bastards. He swore it.

Twenty minutes later, unceremoniously deposited onto a rutted dirt track with two portos, a muledroid, and one daughter, he made that promise overt. He screamed after the fleeing airship, his voice snatched by the wind so that he was certain they couldn't hear a word of it. He screamed anyway.

"You bastards! You miserable, treacherous cowards! I will earn God's blessing and then I will come and find you and pay you back what you deserve you...you...you pirates!"

AIZIKA'S LEGS ACHED. Her shoulders sagged. Her feet felt like they were weeping from a dozen sores and blisters, the wounds thankfully hidden from view by her thick boots. It was cold now, and it hurt to breathe. Her head swam deeper and darker with every step she took. But still they walked.

When they'd been driven off the Behemoth, the sun had still been in its ascent, maybe two fists above the horizon. Now it was two fists above the opposite horizon and sinking fast. Darkness would come soon. Aizika summoned the strength to look ahead, hoping to see some sign of the end. All she saw was a road climbing higher and higher, back and forth up to nowhere. But still they walked.

"Dad, I can't," she gasped as the thin mountain air tore at her throat. "I can't." The porto behind her seemed to voice its assent with a particularly grating whir as it cycled its gear housing.

Her father stopped, glaring back at her with a blend of agitation and annoyance. It felt like he blamed her for everything. She squirmed from one painful foot back to the other, wishing again that it had been him that had gotten sick and not Mother. Eventually, with a withering look at the setting sun, he caved.

"Fine. We can stop for the night by that wreck up there." He nodded towards the next bend, where a rusting hulk was sinking into the cracked and broken road. It looked impossibly far. It also looked like heaven. Wincing through the pain, she trudged onwards.

They'd passed by many such wrecks early on in the march. Aizika, being scared and exhausted, had hardly taken notice. The metal ghosts were nothing but obstacles that forced her off the road, another struggle to overcome in a journey already rife with them.

Now that they were stopping, though—now that she could breathe without her stomach churning and her head swimming through a field of darkness—she gaped in fascination. It was metal, so much metal, at least ten times as large as the portos and muledroid combined. The sight of it was both awe-inspiring and sickening, a testament to the opulence that had defined the previous age. She wondered what it had been used for. Why was it here at all? Her curiosity got the better of her, and she braved a question.

"Was it an angel?" she asked her father as the portos set about unpacking the shelter from the mule droid.

"No," he answered sharply. "At least not one of the true angels. They were sent here to destroy God."

"And they suffered?" she asked, noting the jagged rents in the metal, as if something had stripped it back like an orange peel.

"Yes, they suffered. As they should."

Aizika didn't answer. She instead poked around the wreckage as her father assisted the portos in staking the shelter in place. Her eyes caught on a black metal plate with silver runes carved into it. She wasn't much for reading, and most of it was incomprehensible, but one word of the jumble stood out clearly to her.

"Look, Dad," she called out, "Abrams. Just like you!"

"What?" he said, looking startled. She held out the plate for him to see. He walked over, taking it into his gloved hands. His surprise and worry melted into something even more disconcerting. "Yes, girl," he said, "just like me." He tossed the metal farther down the slope and went back to setting up the shelter.

Once securely inside, he warmed up food from their stores in the muledroid. He ate his fill and then offered her the rest.

She refused. Her stomach felt sour, and her limbs hung uselessly at her side. She was asleep in minutes.

It was not a restful slumber.

"THERE, GIRL," ABRAMS said, unable to keep the excitement from his voice as he pointed a weary finger in front of them. "There, it is them. The Silos!"

He hadn't been sure at first, afraid that his tired eyes were mistaken in what they saw or that his oxygen-starved brain was inventing the vision out of whole cloth. But it was no mistake. There they stood, half a dozen or more structures strewn out along the path, giant spheres of white and metal gleaming in the later afternoon sun. The Enchanted Silos. The home of God. He'd been marching up the mountain for nearly two days straight now, and travelling for much longer, but Abrams's journey was finally at its end. Almost.

"Girl?" he asked when she said nothing. He turned back to see her still clinging atop the muledroid, the cold gray of her eyes boring into him. Her stare was as blank as it was terrifying. Suppressing a shudder, he turned back ahead and marched farther up the cracked and brittle path.

"Where's our sacrifice?" she called out to him.

He froze, his heart pounding in his chest. That question, her eyes.... She knew.

"What?" he asked, feigning ignorance in a hope that it would buy him time.

"Where's our sacrifice?" she pressed again, her voice quiet but strong. "You said we were making the Pilgrimage so we could sacrifice to God and earn a blessing. That's why we loaded all this wood onto the muledroid, right? So where is it? What are we sacrificing?"

"God will provide," he answered, not daring to look back as he resumed his walk. "Up ahead, I'm certain."

"Something lives up this high?"

"God will provide!" he snapped at her, silently cursing his dead wife and the sharp intellect she had passed on to their daughter. "And if not, then we'll scrap one of the portos as a sacrifice instead. Useless fucking things would be worth a damn for once."

Aizika said nothing, her return to silence only confirming that she knew. It was fine. Even if she did know what he planned for her at the summit, there was nothing she could do to stop him. The girl had been unable to walk for hours now, confined by weakness to the back of the muledroid. She couldn't overpower him. She couldn't escape, and even if she could, where would she go?

No, he told himself, her knowing didn't change his plan. If anything, it made it easier. Her caustic petulance, her constant needling, it helped him forget that he'd once held her in his arms or that he'd comforted her when she called out at night. It hardened his heart against what had to come next. The sacrifice would still be unpleasant, but it would be worth it.

He was nearing the summit, muledroid and portos groaning behind him, when he noticed a simple stone altar built into the center of the road. His pulse quickened, and his apprehension melted into excitement. He allowed himself to picture all that would soon be his. Fame, power, riches beyond his wildest dreams, his prize for hearing God's call and proving beyond question his devotion. All it would take was a simple sweep of a knife.

"Come here, girl," he said, greed quickly overcoming a final stab of reluctant regret. Hauling her off of the mule droid, he began dragging her towards the altar.

"What are you doing!" she cried out, her limbs flailing weakly against his grasp.

He thought for a moment of binding her hands but decided against it. What could she do now? His lungs rasping from the effort, he set her down atop the altar, pinning her in place with one hand while the other reached for his knife.

"Sorry, girl," he gasped, forcing himself not to look at her. "I really am. I'm just doing what God told me." The knife slid free of its sheath and he lifted it towards the sky. He'd expected the girl to scream, or to cry, but she did neither. A chill came over him. He finally looked down and saw not terror in her eyes, but defiance. She smiled darkly.

"Holy Gabriel, servant of God, protect me!" she called out with a voice calm and confident.

Abrams moved to plunge the knife into her throat. Before he could, a mighty rush of wind swept the mountaintop, and a steel grip clenched around his wrist. He turned to see a beast of metal had appeared beside him, its wings splaying wide from a glistening copper chest. An angel. Abrams felt his breath leave him.

With a single twitch of its claw-like hands, the angel broke Abrams's wrist. The knife fell. Another blow from the metal creature sent him to his knees.

Aizika freed herself from his grasp, her eyes never leaving his as she went to retrieve the blade. Weapon in hand, she walked back over, her face set in a look of grim determination he knew all too well. He tried to get away, but the angel was too strong.

"Aizika, don't," he pleaded. "Please, I'm...I'm your father."

"You think you're the only one who dreams?" was all she said in reply. The knife flashed briefly in the sunlight as she slammed it home.

WATCHING THROUGH GABRIEL'S camera feed, Gloria Olive Durham smiled as the blood poured from Abram Miller's throat. The girl had done well. Understandably, she'd been terrified when Gloria had visited her in her dreams last night, but she'd listened carefully and spoken the instructed words at the appointed time. Even better, she'd generally kept her wits about her throughout. Perhaps she was finally the one, a worthy heir to a god's legacy.

Because Gloria was getting old. Her gene therapy nanos were still doing a commendable job, but there was no use denying it any longer. Master of the world or not, the one thing she couldn't conquer was her own humanity. She had a decade. Maybe two. She needed to find her replacement. Unfortunately, that task had proven stubbornly difficult. It wasn't enough for her would-be protégé to match her unsurpassable intellect; they needed to see her vision. They needed to understand what the New Kingdom was, what the world could become when governed by a single, all-powerful force. And they needed the steel in their heart to destroy those who would oppose that future.

This one—Aizika Anne Miller—she had promise. The girl's initials might not be as fortuitously grandiose as Gloria's own, and they'd lose at least a year teaching her the basics. She couldn't even read! But Gloria had peered into the girl's soul, and it was a mirror of her own. This could finally be the one. And, if not, she could always be disposed like the others.

As for the father...Gloria smiled, taking a sip of wine. The look of shocked terror on his dying face delivered a thrill she so rarely got to enjoy these days. It was his bewilderment as much as his pain that set her tingling. That he'd ever believed he was worthy of her blessing! Absolutely delightful.

Well, it was about what he deserved. He'd been willing to kill for her favor, so certainly he was willing to lay down his life for the same? Ha! Of course he wasn't. Too bad for him, that's not how deities worked.

She let out a small sigh of satisfaction as she watched the light fade from his eyes, indulging in a second glass of wine. It had been a good day's work. She had found a new protégé, and another martyr had died for his god.

That was, she decided, a most worthy end.

"A MOST WORTHY END" © 2018 by Timothy Shea

T.R. Shea is a writer, veteran, and freelance economist. His speculative fiction examines issues of philosophy and morality in distant futures, drawing heavily from his time in Afghanistan. He currently resides in Hawaii with his wife and dog where they spend their days hiking, snorkeling, and generally enjoying their extended vacation from the US mainland.

A Step Out Into the Blue

by Hilary B. Bisenieks

ELAINE'S STOMACH LEAPED into her throat as the airship dropped into the cloud tops, the sky outside going from blue to gray. Cargo in the hold crashed and scattered when the ship leveled out a moment later, making Elaine glad she'd secured her tool-roll when they'd scrambled to take off a minute before.

Next to her, the little caged navigation demon took a break from its incessant nattering to whimper.

Elaine swore. She shouldn't be here. They should have given her a chance to disembark before leaving the maintenance yard, unfinished installation be damned. Stupid lowlander raiders. With luck, the ship's skeleton crew would be able to repel the barbarians. She muttered a charm to keep herself upright, one of the few pieces of magic her job had taught her, and held her breath.

It was thrilling to be skybound, though, despite the terror. This could be her chance. Once they were back in port, management would have to transfer her and give her more training. Right? She'd threaten to quit, but as far as management was concerned, she was replaceable. The city of Kingston on Cumulus was full of young women just like her: gifted with magical abilities and ready to be suckered into menial labor with the promise of future training.

Any shred of hope of safe return was shattered as something thumped against the hull, making the ship lurch. Boarders. It couldn't be anything else. The airship pitched, like the pilot was trying to buck the lowlander flier off, like this was some sort of fast attack flier, not a hulking great transport still half-loaded with medical supplies.

The demon whimpered again.

She banged on its cage. "Hush up! I don't like this any more than you do." If the little bastard hadn't been so hard to corral in the first place, maybe Elaine would've gotten to the job on time and finished installing the demon before the lowlanders showed up. She should be sneaking around the academy after skiving of work right now, trying to learn more magery rather than wondering if she'd make it home alive.

Stupid job. If they would just give her the training she'd been promised for months, Elaine could've quit and gotten a real mage's job instead. Something safe and away from the maintenance yard and its lax security.

The ship lurched with a second thump. In the distance, someone shouted. Then gunshots rang out.

The airship burst through the cloud- tops, sunlight lancing through the porthole above Elaine's head, then leveled out.

More shouting. More shooting.

There was no place for Elaine to hide in the relay room. The space was little more than a closet lined with a mess of pipes and crystals that shunted power and control signals between the bridge and the ship's engines and lift units. If she wanted to avoid being shot by a lowlander, she'd have to find somewhere else.

The narrow corridor outside was empty for the moment. Elaine didn't know much about the layout of the ship—she'd mostly done installs on smaller, merchant-class vessels, not these military supply ships—but she'd passed an entrance to the hold on her way aboard. The lowlanders would look there at some point, but hopefully they wouldn't do too thorough of a search until they'd set the ship down someplace. It wasn't a great idea, but it wasn't like she had a better plan.

Elaine grabbed her tool-roll and crept out of the relay room and down the corridor, shutting the door against the nav demon's protests as softly yet swiftly as she could. She stifled a yelp at a sudden noise behind her and dashed the rest of the way to the hold, expecting at any moment to hear a gunshot or a shout, but nothing happened.

In the hold, the cargo was scattered across the deck from their evasive maneuvers. The ship was supposed to stop over in the maintenance yard just long enough for Elaine to install the nav demon before moving on. It shouldn't have even been loaded to begin with. Nevertheless, the chaos of the hold was a godsend.

Elaine found a hiding spot among some pallets of bandages beneath a heavy tarp where she could still see the doorway. From there, she might be able to manage a stunning spell. She knew the words for one at any rate. If it came to a fight, her chances weren't good, but at least in the hold, she had some space to move and evade.

She hadn't been pursued into the hold, and the shooting had stopped. Maybe the lowlanders had been repelled? Elaine didn't know how large a crew had been aboard when they had taken off, nor how many lowlanders had been in pursuit.

A shadow passed across the sliver of hallway outside, and a moment later, a woman stepped through the door. She had commanding bearing, definitely not one of the ship's original crew. So much for that hope.

The woman wore a motley but dashing ensemble that looked like it had been pillaged from half the sky's armies: her breeches, blouse, and vest a riot of contrasting colors, topped with a long, heavy coat that nearly brushed the floor. In one hand, she bore a carbine like those used by air crews around the maintenance yard, while her other hand gripped a tall staff that she seemed to lean on slightly.

A mage's staff. Its power tingled at the edge of Elaine's perception.

Had this lowlander stolen a mage's staff, or was she herself a mage? The woman stalked through the hold. She didn't carry herself like any of the mages Elaine had met—no haughtiness in her dress or her step. But she didn't look like the pictures of barbaric lowlanders from the papers, either.

The woman passed within a few feet of Elaine's hiding spot, and Elaine prayed she could hold herself still enough. She could cast an illusion to hide further, but not without making a sound. The officer walked on, though, step, thump, her footfalls and the sound of the staff hitting the deck the only sounds in Elaine's world. Then, satisfied, the woman left, and Elaine could breathe again.

Elaine stayed put, wondering what she should do. It was a foolhardy thought, but if she could steal the staff, surely even her meager abilities would allow her to send some sort of distress signal. The chances of her being able to steal it, whether the lowlander was mage or simple pirate, were slim.

If she had the demon, though... Its abilities were limited, but with luck and maybe some coaxing, Elaine might be able to use it to get a message out.

One of the first spells that Elaine had taught herself was a silencing charm. It made it easier to sneak around the mage's academy and get bits and pieces of the training she'd otherwise been denied. It came in handy now, as she extricated herself from under the tarp and crossed the hold.

The ship had sunk back into the cloud layer, though the smoothness of its flight suggested they were yet near the top, and the shadows in the corridor outside had lost some of their definition.

She eased open the door to the relay room and peeked inside, the effort of maintaining her silencing charm for so long draining on her. Indeed, the room was quiet once Elaine entered and closed the door. She released her silencing charm, feeling the weight of maintaining it lift from her shoulders, and she breathed deeply for a few moments, her back against the door.

It wasn't until she took another look around the room after collecting herself that Elaine realized why the room was so quiet. The nav demon, who had nattered at her quietly in its own language nearly constantly since she'd collected it from the office on her way to this job, was gone. The lowlander officer. She must have taken it while she was searching the ship.

The demon wasn't smart, exactly—it could replace a human navigator, and it knew how to keep altitude and heading for the ship if the pilot stepped away from the helm—but Elaine didn't doubt for a moment that it would give her up, her presence if not her location, the moment it felt threatened. They already knew she was aboard, then.

Using the demon to send a distress signal had been her best plan, but another option remained. A desperate option, built on chance and hope, though little of either. The mage's staff.

Elaine didn't know if the lowlander captain used it for its magical power or just for the power that it implied, but if Elaine could get it, the power that it held would make up for her own lack of talent. With the staff, she could get home, and they'd have to train her. She'd make them do it.

The ship began to shake a little, buffeted by turbulent winds. They were sinking lower into the cloud layer.

Slowly, Elaine got to her feet and listened at the door. If she could keep her balance, the creaking of wood around her should obviate her need to use the silencing charm again for a while, anyway. After a moment's consideration, she also got out the biggest of her wrenches. With the element of surprise, it might serve her better than trying to use an unfamiliar spell.

Once again Elaine stepped into the corridor, ears straining to hear footsteps over the sounds of wind and wood. She stayed low, each step careful as she headed towards the bridge. It had sounded like at least two flyers had landed on the airship, but who knew if either remained, or if they'd departed, leaving behind a prize crew?

Elaine saw the first bullet hole as she reached the end of the corridor—a jagged, splintered scar in the wall. She peered

around the corner but saw only more bullet holes, empty shell
casings, and a splash of blood.

The air reeked of gunpowder, smoke still hanging in the air.
Light lanced through a bullet hole in the far wall.

Elaine took shallow breaths as she moved down the corridor towards the door to the bridge, expecting at any moment
to hear someone shouting at her from behind, or the crack of a
gunshot.

The door to the bridge was closed, but over the sound of
the wind outside, Elaine could hear a voice. She inched her way
towards the door and put an eye up to a bullet hole in the wall
by the doorframe.

The lowlander officer was inside, seated at the controls.
Elaine's limited view, however, didn't show her anyone else. Or
the nav demon or the staff.

Elaine pressed her ear to the hole just in time to hear a
quick "Yes, Captain Barton," then footsteps approaching. She
dared a glance through the hole, just long enough to see that
someone else, a young woman, on the bridge, was coming towards the door. Elaine looked left and right, and then moved
to the other side of the door so that she would be between the
door and the wall when it opened.

With a tremendous effort, she muttered the words for an
illusion, followed by her silencing charm. A real mage would be
able to weave a tapestry of light and dark to perfectly conceal
anything they wished or simply turn themselves invisible.

Elaine turned the color of the wall behind her.

A moment later, the door swung open, nearly slamming
into Elaine's head, and the young woman walked out, passing

down the corridor and around the corner without so much as a glance back.

Still on silenced feet, Elaine exhaled and slipped around the door.

The bridge was clean, save for a few splinters of wood from the bullet hole in the wall behind her and some shards of glass where the bullet had come to rest in one of the gauges. The huge panoramic window that dominated the far side of the bridge was undamaged.

And the captain's chair was empty.

A tingle of power and the lightest touch of something cold accompanied a steely voice. "Can I help you with something, little one?"

Elaine shook her head, suddenly unable to find her words.

"Turn around nice and slow, and let's have a look at you," Captain Barton commanded.

Elaine complied. Her gaze skated around the wall as Barton looked her over, finally settling on the splintered bullet hole. What would it feel like to be shot, she wondered? Or would they even waste a bullet on her? They could just toss Elaine overboard and let gravity do the work.

"What are you doing here?" Barton asked.

Elaine stammered, trying to come up with a convincing lie, wondering what it mattered if she was just going to be killed or sold into slavery.

"Speak." The captain didn't so much point her staff at Elaine as incline it with practiced confidence.

Captain Barton's command didn't feel harsh, for all that her words were cold. Elaine felt the magic course through her, a sort of warmth that brought the truth to her lips. "I was aboard, installing a nav demon, when your flyers were spotted, and I wasn't given a chance to disembark before the ship took off."

"We found your nav demon. What I'm more interested in, though, is what you were doing right here."

Elaine paused for a moment. Again, Barton inclined her staff a fraction of an inch, and the warmth washed through Elaine. "I saw you with your staff when I was hiding in the hold. I was going to use the demon to send a distress signal, but then I found it gone."

"You wanted to steal my staff, then?"

Elaine nodded.

"Not the wisest plan, but you were clever enough to evade us for this long. And you've a bit of talent to you already." She nodded. "You could be of use."

"Of use?" Elaine blanched. She'd almost rather be killed. Better dead than enslaved to barbaric lowlanders.

"Sit." The power she put through Elaine wasn't violent, but it lacked the warmth of the earlier compulsion. "And put that wrench away. We both know it wouldn't have done you any good."

Elaine's feet took her to one of the chairs beside the captain's, her knees bent, and she sat. She opened her tool-roll and replaced the wrench. When she'd only been compelled to speak, Barton's power had felt like a warm tingle, gently leading her to do the right thing. This, though—Elaine felt cold, disconnected from her whole body.

"You'll stay there and not make trouble, I trust?" Barton asked. "I can make you comply, but I find that tiresome."

Elaine nodded. Anything to avoid that cold power that severed her from her own will.

Barton seated herself at the ship's controls and pulled the speaking horn towards herself. "Nell, you can come back now. I've found our stowaway."

They could be going anywhere, flying through the cloud layer, but Captain Barton, checking against the binnacle, seemed confident of their heading.

Nell appeared a few minutes later, scowling at Elaine. She and Barton had a quick whispered conversation in a Slavic-sounding language, which led to more scowling before Nell stalked off, muttering.

The ship dipped below the clouds, revealing a scorched landscape. Elaine hadn't realized that they'd flown far enough to reach one of the Exterminations. Nothing moved below them. Nothing lived. The whole of the earth's surface, for hundreds of miles, littered here and there with the hulking great bones of impossible beasts, was burned, salted, and poisoned so that nothing would grow.

In the distance, though, there seemed to be some variation, some patch of color breaking up the grays and blacks and browns.

"I won't be your slave," Elaine said, her eyes fixed on that patch of color on the horizon. "I think I'd rather be left here to fend for myself."

The captain laughed. "Slave? Really? Is that what people are saying about us nowadays?"

"You said that I could be 'of use,'" Elaine said, reddening at Barton's laughter. Did this lowlander take her for a fool? Well, if she did, that wasn't wholly unfair. Elaine had tried to steal a mage's staff.

"I did, and you can," Barton said. "If you want to. You could be trained, work a job that you enjoy. Or you can be returned to your former life, if that's what you'd prefer. That's not what I would choose, though, if I were you."

"Really," Elaine said, feeling somehow safe to let sarcasm edge into her voice. "Because from where I'm sitting, it still feels like I'm being kidnapped. Anyway, what do you know of my life?"

Captain Barton turned and looked Elaine dead in the eyes. "You've got talent that's going to waste. You work a dead-end job in the hopes that one day you'll get the chance to climb the ladder, get some training, and do something better. The rich are robbing you blind and telling you you're lucky to have as much as you do. I'd trade that away in an instant."

Elaine's eyes widened, then narrowed. "And I suppose that I'd be better off among barbarians and pirates, scraping out a living on the surface, always on the lookout for some hulking great monster who could come along and eat me up like a snow pea?"

"You really don't know anything about what it's like down on the surface, do you? Only the propaganda they've been feeding you since the day of your birth."

The patch of color on the horizon was somewhat larger than before, though without any sense of speed or scale, Elaine couldn't guess how long it would be until they reached it. "I suppose that you're going to tell me that it's a fantasyland where nothing bad happens? You're going to say that nobody from the surface ever forms a raiding party, boards a cargo ship, kills her crew, and kidnaps a young woman who shouldn't even be aboard, for instance? Try the other one, it's got bells."

"Believe me or don't," Barton said, looking again at Elaine. "We'll be landing in less than an hour's time. If you're convinced that you'd be better off back where you came from, I'll personally see to it that you're put on a flyer and left somewhere safe with a distress beacon and a week's worth of food. I was like you, once." She carefully pulled one sleeve up, revealing a mass of taut, scarred skin covering half of her forearm. Above it, there was part of a faded tattoo, its blue-black lines describing some sort of regimental insignia.

"Before I went to the surface, I served the Queen. I was a mage for the Fifth Heavy Dragoons, fighting for queen and country above the continent."

The captain fell silent, and for a minute, there was only the sound of engines and wind.

Elaine broke the silence at last. "What happened to make you leave?"

"My platoon's flyer was shot down near Zagreb. Nobody else survived. I barely did. Some civilians pulled me out of the fire, helped patch me up.

"I could have gone back. I could have laid a beacon on myself and brought my own rescue, gone home to medals. But I saw something. Those refugees, living on the surface? They had nothing. Nobody but themselves to rely on. Zagreb, high overhead, was not their home. The occupying forces had made certain of that. But they kept going. There was talk among them of a safe haven, so I decided that I'd help them get there."

Captain Barton lapsed into silence again. After a few minutes, Elaine felt compelled to ask, "Then what happened?"

"We got picked up by a crew out searching for refugees and taken to a camp. I stayed. Not there, ultimately. But the lead-

ers of that camp had already scouted out several locations for
us to move to. By the time that location was no longer tenable,
everything was set for us to up and move to another place."

Silence, again. "So you're taking me to, what? A refugee
camp?"

"Yes. And no. Freiheit isn't just a camp, though we have
people trying to find refugees, still. The war isn't just the glory
you read about in the papers. Nobody talks about the human
toll on those uninvolved citizens around whose ears the wars
keep descending, I bet. I certainly didn't think about any of
that until some of those very people saved me."

A thought struck Elaine. "What happened to the crew?
The guys you stole this ship from?"

"They're safe, I promise."

"Like hell they are! I saw bullet holes. I saw blood! I may
have been a bit of a fool trying to get your staff, but I'm not stupid."

"Look," Barton said, pointing to a ragged, bloody hole in
one leg of her trousers. No wonder she'd been leaning on her
staff earlier. "The only person shot was me. This ship's former
crew were put on flyers, unconscious but unharmed, and left
somewhere they'd be found. Just as you would have been, if
we'd found you when we first boarded. That's as far as I can
vouch for their safety."

Elaine gave her a skeptical look. This Captain Barton certainly wasn't like any of the lowlanders she'd ever heard about.
Hell, she couldn't think of anyone who would make an effort
not to harm people who were shooting at them.

"I didn't start my day looking to kidnap anyone," Barton
said, seeming to read her mind. "But here you are. Your being

here is my mistake, and I've got to take some responsibility for that. We're not the bloodthirsty pirates that your serials and newspapers make us out to be. The women and men of Freiheit aren't anyway. We take what we need, as payment for the violence that's been done to our people by society and wars, but we don't take lives. Not if we can help it."

"Alright, say I come to Freiheit," Elaine said. "And say I don't take you up on the offer of safe transport away. What did you mean about training?"

"As a mage," the captain said. "There are precious few of us around. Those charms to turn you colors and silence your footfalls were well done for someone with little training. Just think what you could do if you were apprenticed to an actual mage."

"Really?" Elaine's heart leaped, then sank. Training, yes. That was what she had wanted, what she'd begged for, but like this? Leaving behind all that she knew up in the sky? The other girls from the boarding house would wonder what happened to her. Maybe some of them would miss her. "What happens if I want to leave? Later, I mean?"

"Anyone in Freiheit is free to leave, so long as they don't mean us harm. The council might decide to bind you to certain promises, if you did decide to leave. Many of us are thieves of a sort, after all. Anyhow, think it over. We arrive in half an hour."

"And if there are any affairs I need to wrap up, back where I'm from?"

Barton gave her a critical look. "You resent your job, where they likely pay you pittance, so you live in a boarding house with other girls, sorry, women, like yourself. If you had any family attachments, you would have mentioned them already. How am I doing?"

Elaine glared at her.

"The offer I make to you is sincere, but it's not the offer I would make to everybody. Living in Freiheit is an adjustment, and it's not one that everyone can make."

The patch of color in the distance had grown so that Elaine could now see it for what it was: a city, fortified and vibrant, in the midst of one of the Exterminations. There, below the cloud layer, there was life, greenery, even. It seemed such an unlikely sight, though she knew that people had lived on the surface for countless millennia.

"If I do stay, and I'm not saying that I will, but if I do, can I send word back, at least to let some of the others at the boarding house know I'm safe?"

Barton's face softened a touch, and she nodded. "If you stay, of course. We have our ways."

"Thank you."

If...

It would be a change, but wasn't that what Elaine had been wanting? And Captain Barton had said that she could always go home if she chose to.

Somehow, Elaine knew that wasn't what her choice would be.

Hilary B. Bisenieks is a Philadelphian, a sysadmin, and a Hufflepuff. He lives in Oakland with his wife and two cats. His fiction has appeared most recently in LampLight Magazine. Hi-

lary can be found online at hilarybisenieks.com and on Twitter, where he tweets at @HBBisenieks.

Lips of Red, Lips of Black

by A. J. Hackwith

IT TOOK THREE BONE mages and a dreadnaught with a terrorsoul to capture the paper pirate Katha. A crown of stolen reliquary shards, worth half a ship each, still nettled her dark hair as she came, barefoot and snarling, before the Lady of Embers.

The dreadnaught was the Lady's, and she its captain. All of the Isles knew it. She'd given her own fear to fuel its skyheart, and now had none left of her own. Each ship required a sacrifice of its captain to fly, a desire, an emotion, a fate. Ships with terrorsouls were fast and feared, as were their captains.

So all Isles know the Lady's ways were not kind, especially to one of her own. But through coal and spike, the pirate Katha had one refrain: "Just wait until my true love comes."

"Your crew is dead. Your friends have flown," the Lady said, as she split Katha's lip and placed a traitor's brand upon her skin. "You'll die for what you've stolen from me."

And Katha's smile was red touched with iron blood. "Just wait until my true love comes."

"To the decks," the Lady instructed her women, and on an eight-armed skyhook beast they flew. Collared mages bound Katha to a pillar on the rusting deck, a pyre of cold straw to warm her toes. Smoke clogged the Isle of Embers in a sooty fog and stained her lips with ash. A taste before the flames.

Yet Katha said, "Just wait until my true love comes."

"All you love is lost and so are you," said the Lady. "I burned your ship, you foolish thing, and I'll do you just the same. Who dares to fly a paper ship in the realm of flames?"

Katha, bloodied, burned, and bound, laughed high and loud. The wind picked up, guttering torchfire. The flecks of black in the wind coalesced, a wing of ash pierced through the gloom. There rose a black cloud, a wyrm, a myth of ash and sail. Light speared the deck, wind swept the straw away. The dreadnaught swayed as cannons rose, under fire from a ship of shadow and lightning.

"She still flies." The paper pirate's hands were free, but the Lady of Embers wreathed herself in flame.

"I burned your ship and branded your skin, you have no way to fly," the Lady said. "There's no sky for a branded soul."

"Aye, that might be, if it was me who captained her." The vessel was a blot of sky, ink and fury laced with bone-white fire. Soot settled on Katha's brow. She turned her face into it like a kiss as she mounted the railing. "But even you should know, paper does not make a ship, as flesh doesn't make a soul. There's better fuel than fear."

Iron buckled and rust wept down. The Lady of Embers threw fire at a futile sky, and the ash prow embraced it whole. "Impossible! No fool can sacrifice her heart to the sky and still live."

And at that, Katha paused, one foot over open air. Flames licked her boot but were ignored. Flame and ash seemed nothing to one who grieved. "That's what I told her," she said. "That's the thing about love—it doesn't care."

Storm-wrought light lashed out from the ghost ship, piercing the dreadnaught's terrorsoul. An empire of fear returned to its captain like a flood in a dry creek bed. The Lady of Embers ignited the sky as she went down.

And Katha leapt to a ship of paper ash. She stroked a charred railing, for there was no wheel to steer, and pressed her sooted fingertips to her mouth. The skyheart flew where it wanted, brittle and burning and bright.

"Burn that horizon, love," she whispered. The ship took the sky on ash-eaten hearts, and Katha's smile was black.

A.J. Hackwith is a magpie of ink, bad ideas, and spite. She's a queer writer of fantasy and science fiction in Seattle. A.J. is the author of two non-fiction books and writes sci-fi romance as Ada Harper. You can find her as @ajhackwith on Twitter and other dark corners of the internet.

Every Subject's Soul Is Her Own

by Kelly Rossmore

AN AMERICAN CHICA CROONING about love filtered in from the radio in the corner as First Mate Maria Estrella Gutierrez slid into a rickety chair at one of the tables of the dingy bar. Across from her in a striped men's suit sat her former best friend, a former person, too, according to los locos. Some people believed that the gears and bolts they installed in place of eyes and bits she'd rather not think about meant that a Compass like Emilia was no longer a human being.

All the air pinched out of her chest as she forced herself to look at her friend. Gears turned under what remained of the dark skin at her neck as Emilia cocked her head at Maria, her mechanical eyes blinking slowly and with an audible click.

Dios, it was a blessing that the American music and the conversations from the half-filled Havana bar drowned out the rest of the sounds from Emilia's augmented Compass body. Metal replaced half the skin on her arms, glinting yellow under the cheap lights, and there were couplings on the palms of her unnaturally still brown hands, which rested on the beer-stained table.

She missed Emilia's dark eyes, the way the old lamps of the neglected streets they'd grown up on in Santiago had rendered them luminous, reflecting her friend's girlish dreams for a better life. A life where they'd still have each other, Cuba would be free, and they'd have a permanent roof above their heads.

"Maria," Emilia said, her head still cocked. The thick curls she'd once sported would've covered the gears in her neck, but had been replaced now by a short cap. "You asked for me?"

It was her voice, the medical mechanics of Guantanamo Bay hadn't changed that, but it was foreign in all other ways. Emilia spoke in the precise and emotionless English of Compasses instead of the rapid, fiery Spanish of their youth.

"I wanted to see you," Maria said, surprised to discover it was the simple truth.

For years she hadn't, paralyzed by her own guilt and afraid to see what her friend had become. But her life had become stacked with regrets, and she'd acquired a growing need to shorten that stack.

"You want me on your ship," Emilia said. "They say your last job fue una tragedia."

Emilia's voice was still flat, so Maria reined in her hope at the mixing of Spanish with English, something many of their Cuban people did these days en una rebelión pequeña against the American occupation.

"Sí," Maria said, encouraging her as if they were young girls again. "Te necesito. Por favor."

Emilia frowned, though with those mechanical eyes Maria could no longer read how she really felt. Or if she felt the same about anything anymore, Maria thought, pain lurching in her chest again. Had it all been for nothing?

"Bueno," was all Emilia said, though. "What do you need?"
"I need you to remember," said Maria.

FROM THE DECK OF THE American airship Justice, Maria gazed out across the dockyards of Havana Harbor. Far more crowded than even ten years ago, the harbor currently had a dozen airships of various sizes docked, while beyond them countless seagoing ships of every size bobbed in the water. The Justice was of average dimensions for an airship, lightly gunned but surprisingly swift and maneuverable;: an ideal scout ship. All the airships and the large military sea vessels before her were American, not Cuban, and more appeared each year.

After helping Cuba finally oust Spain at the turn of the century, the United States had offered a big brotherly hand in setting up a new government on the island. Motivas ulteriores emerged in the years after, though, as the US expanded their airship construction operations at Guantanamo to assert control over the shipping lanes of the Americas and later in response to the first outbreak of world war in Europe.

With world war brewing there once again, America's demand for airships and the Compasses necessary to operate them had swelled even higher in the last few years.

So had its need to exert political influence over Cuba in the name of protecting its assets. Cuba's freedom had been a brief spark in a long history of occupation, extinguished once again.

"Gutierrez! Get over here," Captain Fred Connors said, his gringo accent butchering Maria's name again across the deck.

Shaped like the hull of an old European warship, the airship Justice was lighter, able to be lifted by the massive balloons above it and powered by an engine whose secrets the US kept under wraps from Cubans—except for Compasses like Emilia. Whatever the engine did, a human had to be augmented to control it.

The captain held court above her at the ship's sterncastle, while Maria stood on the main deck helping the Cuban crew load wooden boxes of supplies onto the Justice. Maria threw down a rope with more force than needed and climbed up the stairs with what she hoped was a neutral expression.

Women weren't looked at favorably for crewing airships or becoming the Compasses that piloted them, but orphans like Maria and Emilia with neither family to care about them nor white enough beauty had been allowed to volunteer for the new and highly dangerous airship prototypes and Compass transformations. Maria knew lucky timing—volunteering when so few would—and persistence had been everything. And even so, within the American airship fleet, she knew she was fortunate to have risen to first mate; she could go no higher.

"Yes, Captain?" she said once she'd joined him, unsurprised to see the captain's lapdog, one of the two American engineers, standing with Captain Connors on the sterncastle.

Through the closed doors behind them lay the navigation room, where Maria had left Emilia checking the equipment earlier. This included the strange machine Emilia would soon connect herself into that regulated the engine, a contraption with gears and pumps and mechanical slots to place her arms and her face, and viewing lenses that lined up with her artificial eyes.

"She couldn't have been the only Compass you could find," the captain said, staring her down. In his polished American uniform with his imposing height and receding sandy brown hair, it was a stern look bien practicada.

Maria was also well- practiced in withstanding it. "Compasses travel up into the sky, Captain. They do not fall from it."

"Sometimes they do, with the rest of us." The black humor triggered a boyish grin that softened his usually harsh demeanor. "Since our last one vanished without a sign, I'd say we're due for one to tumble into our laps."

Maria understood why the Americans had made him a captain. He wielded that infectious grin well, aware how a joke at the right moment and a determined attitude could inspire his subordinates. It didn't overcome the whole, however. "I spoke to several Compasses," she replied, "and there were reservations. What happened on our last voyage is known."

His frown intensified, as she'd expected it would, which helped cover up her lie. She'd approached only Emilia.

"I thought those automatons couldn't feel anything," he said, before turning to his lapdog engineer. "I never understood why they weren't declared military assets. We'd be assigned one then as needed, without a damn hunt."

She imagined the Compasses she'd worked with, all Cuban citizens who'd allowed their bodies and minds to be fractured in a sacrifice of self, handed around like objects. Hatred burned hot inside her.

Of course his perrito engineer was quick to agree in a meaningless pageant of words, but Captain Connors soon brought his attention back to Maria. With an air of granting her a favor when in reality there was no time to find another Compass before their scheduled patrol, he said, "Fine, we'll see how she does. We depart in the morning. Get the crew ready."

He looked up and down Maria's thin, deeply suntanned body in the crew jumpsuit, topped by a short mop of wild dark hair. His lip curled. "You would hire the Negro woman Compass though."

She said nothing, because there was nothing polite to say. Just another *herida* upon endless ones.

AS THEY WERE THE ONLY two women on board, Maria was unsurprised when Captain Connors told her to share her quarters with Emilia. When her friend entered the tiny first-mate's cabin that night, Maria asked, "We're set?"

Emilia leaned against the closed door, the gray jumpsuit she wore similar to Maria's blue one, except hers had zippered sleeves that allowed Compasses to swiftly conquer a wayward engine. Her mouth curved upwards to form the same shy smile present in so many of Maria's best memories. "Sí, todo es listo. Vive José Martí."

Maria grinned at her friend so wide her cheeks ached. They'd grown up near one of the many monuments to Cuba's fallen patriot. She'd feared that after years of working as a Compass, Emilia would've forgotten the plan or resented her for changing the script. They had vowed to do everything together, but at the last moment before undergoing the surgery to become a Compass, Maria had lost her courage. Ever since, she'd sworn never to let fear control her again.

"I've missed you." Maria closed most of the gap between them, but not all. She didn't know how her friend felt about her anymore.

"The surgery," Emilia said haltingly, her usually distant voice collecting more emotion as she spoke. "You forget so much. Your memories, how to talk. Some of us forget how to walk, too. We always have to think carefully about how to form words right."

Maria closed her eyes in pain for a moment. That explained why most Compasses she'd met spoke as they did.

"From before, I remember fragments," Emilia said. "You were in most of them. Enough of the plan was there, too, so it was familiar. I just needed you to remind me."

"We've been apart so long." Maria pushed herself to say it. "Do you hate me?"

Emilia cocked her head like she had back in the bar in Havana. "Why would I?" She gestured at Maria and then herself. "Familia. Para siempre."

"Para siempre," Maria whispered in return as they always had, her vision blurring. She hugged her friend, ignoring the whirl of gears near her ear and a patch of cool metal against her cheek.

Strong arms encircled her, and soft words sank deep into Maria's soul. "I'm glad you didn't do it."

Maria's next breath emerged ragged. The immense burden she'd grown so accustomed to carrying was crumbling away, a relief beyond words, and yet its loss also left her raw and exposed.

When they pulled apart, Emilia seemed to pull back emo-tionally, too, her face more remote. "The plan works like this anyway," she said. She sat down on the bed and encouraged Maria to join her with a stiff pat of her augmented hand. "Let's review the details."

SINCE THE AMERICANS prohibited Cuban crew from possessing any handheld firearms for "safety," Maria's smuggler contact in Havana had marked the boxes carrying the hidden guns with a splash of red paint. Two days after liftoff, near dawn, Maria distributed the weapons to the Cuban crew members.

One engineer they cornered down in the engine room with the threat of knives and fists, because no one would risk firing a shot there. Once he was secured with rope in the cargo hold, Maria directed her men to round up the few American sympa-thizers among the crew and lock them up with the engineer.

A pistol in her hand, she crept down the cramped hallway to the perrito engineer's room. His lapdog ways had granted him the second best cabin on the ship, directly below the cap-tain's. She'd chosen dawn because it was a rare time of day when the two men were apart; they often drank and talked long into the night.

Two of the crew stood just behind her. While all were armed, she'd reminded them they needed the engineer alive. She knocked on the locked door, and curses and grumbling erupted from inside. "It's not my shift!"

"Open up. I need to talk to you."

The door opened, and the man's unshaven, bitter face changed to shock when he absorbed the sight of the three of them, guns in hand. She pushed inside before he could prevent it, her men following. Still in his rumpled clothes from the day before, the engineer backed away toward the bed, stumbling over the pants, shirts and utensils scattered across the floor of the cluttered cabin. He snatched up a broom from the corner as if to ward them off with it.

"Come quietly, perro," one of her men said. He held the rope to tie him with.

The engineer looked up. Catching his thought instantly, Maria rushed toward him. She was too late.

"Captain! Mutiny!" he yelled, banging the top of the broom against the ceiling above him.

When she closed in on him, he shoved the broom into her, wielding it like a staff. It sent her tumbling onto the basura-filled floor. She raised her pistol, intending only to threaten with it, but the crack of a shot sounded from behind her.

Blood blossomed high up in the engineer's chest. He stumbled back into a chest of drawers, staring at the bloody hand he'd pressed to his wound. The forgotten broom slipped from his other hand.

"Idiota," she said, glaring at the pale face of the crewman who'd shot him. The plan was to not kill anyone, especially the engineers. She removed the gun from the crewman's limp hand and said, "Get him downstairs. Have the medics look at him."

There were two medics among the crew. Her men carried the engineer out into the hallway, where they encountered Emilia. Maria handed her the gun she'd taken from the man who couldn't be trusted with it.

Her friend grasped it awkwardly, and Maria wordlessly showed Emilia how she held her pistol. Emilia copied her, saying, "The captain heard that. Does he have a radio in his cabin?"

"A small one, perhaps. The communications room is still secure?" It had been Emilia's task to take it over and guard it, with the help of some crew.

"Sí. I left three men there."

"Bueno, we must go quickly then. Before he talks to anyone out there."

They hurried upstairs and then moved more quietly as they neared the captain's door. Listening, she heard him saying, "This is Captain Connors of the airship Justice. Mutiny! We require assistance. Anyone there?"

"Pretend you need help," Emilia whispered in her ear.

No, Maria hadn't completely hidden her dislike for him. He'd rightfully believe she was part of the mutiny. "You just joined us. You do it," she whispered back.

Emilia stuffed the gun into her waistband at her back, her untucked shirt covering it, then knocked on the locked door. "Captain? The crew are acting strange. Should we change course?"

Footsteps thudded on wood as he moved close to the door. "Tell me what they're doing."

"They carried one engineer away. Down the stairs. And they were looking for someone. Perhaps me?" Emilia spoke in her flat Compass voice, as if it had little to do with her. "I hear them now. Getting closer."

Maria tightened her grip on the pistol, waiting. A moment passed in silence. Would the captain risk opening his door to secure the ship's Compass? He moved around the cabin, then returned to the door. "Get in," he said, and it creaked open.

From her hidden position beside the doorway, Maria couldn't see inside. She followed after Emilia almost blindly, only to see the captain grab her friend's arm and pull her aside, a gun to her head. "Lock the door," he told Maria.

Her pulse racing along with her mind, she obeyed him. Her palm was sweating, and it was harder to hang onto the pistol one-handed as she manipulated the door lock.

"Just as I thought," Captain Connors said once she faced him again. "You two know each other."

Maria's gaze met Emilia's artificial eyes, doing their slow blink. Her face was neutral, but her body was twisted away from his, resisting as he used her as a shield. So he wouldn't feel the gun at her waist, Maria realized. He'd had no chance to search her.

He pressed the gun barrel closer to Emilia, who leaned her head away from it as best she could. "Drop the weapon, or I'll shoot her."

She couldn't lose Emilia. To avoid that, she had to use her mind.

"An airship needs its Compass," Maria pointed out. "You can't shoot her."

"Yes, I can." He lowered the gun near Emilia's hip instead. "We aren't too far out. One session, maybe two, should be enough to regulate the engine. We can fly the rest of the way on manual control."

It was true. He could maim Emilia and finish her off later without endangering the ship. If he had his engineers, which he didn't, and a way to send for emergency help in manually docking the ship, which he did.

The small radio he'd been using was on his neatly ordered desk, clear in her line of sight. She'd been pointing her gun at the floor while he had Emilia, but she raised it now, telegraphing how much she wanted to shoot him. He smirked, angling his body sideways to be a smaller target, with Emilia between them.

She shifted her aim slowly to the right, as if giving up the idea, then shot the radio.

"Son of a bitch," he swore, his face reddening when he realized what she'd done.

"We have the ship," she told him. "We have the engineers, and any crew that supported you. There's no one left to help you."

Emilia joined in. "Surrender. You'll be kept alive and safe, then traded later and freed."

A minute ticked by, a bead of sweat trickling down Maria's face as she wondered whether he'd lash out like a cornered rat or yield to reason. The delay also allowed doubts to surface. Her aim was mediocre, poor enough that she wouldn't risk hitting Emilia. If he didn't back down, she had no plan forward.

The captain finally made a decision, an unhappy one judging from the scowl on his face. "All right," he said, releasing his grip on Emilia's arm, and Maria's shoulders loosened in relief.

Then he shoved Emilia hard at Maria, knocking them both against the door. Her pistol wound up pinned between it and Emilia's body, useless as he raised his gun again. She turned to shield Emilia from him, only to feel and hear the jolt of a gun going off right next to her.

Emilia had reached for her hidden weapon while falling onto Maria, turned, and fired, her arm braced against Maria's ribs. Three shots she fired, and only one hit the captain, but it was enough for his bullets to land high, buried in the door above Maria's head. He ducked behind a small table meant for dining and knocked it over for better cover. Blood droplets decorated his path.

The captain released a torrent of curses under his breath, at them and at himself for taking this job.

"There's nowhere to go," Maria said. "Drop your weapon."

"Fine," he said, the word ground out as if through metal. He spat on the floor and hurled one last insult at her.

He'd be more useful to them alive, she reminded herself. After making them swear again that he would not be killed, the captain kicked his gun across the cabin floor. He ignored both them and his wounded shoulder, as if it were all beneath him, as she commanded some of her crew to transport him to the hold with the others. His injury was treated, but the engineer had not survived.

Maria had thought of this day so many times. Un día de triunfo y felicidad. Instead she was exhausted and hollow, and shaky with how narrowly they'd escaped death.

Until she looked at Emilia, who curved an arm around her and smiled, head cocked. "Where shall we go, Captain?"

Anywhere, except there was a grander plan in motion. She'd already smuggled a Compass over to the Resistance, and now she had an airship.

"Wherever Cuba needs us," she told Emilia. "So we can all be free."

The war was just beginning. Today was the birthday of José Martí, beloved poet and patriot, with the uprising on the Justice echoed by citizens all across Cuba. Unlike the revolutions before it, this one was taking place not only in the fields and mountains and cities, but across the skies above.

"EVERY SUBJECT'S SOUL is Her Own" © 2018 by Kelly Rossmore

Kelly Rossmore likes stories about faraway worlds and in the real world enjoys snapping photos of her travels. She also flexes her number -crunching powers, writes, games, and pets her needy cats. She is a graduate of the Viable Paradise writing workshop. Follow her on Twitter as @Sybara.

Thou Shalt Be Free As Mountain Winds

by Jennifer Mace

THE LAST TIME I SAW Aly, we were chasing a different sunset.

I hadn't known it was the last, of course. We used to chase them all the time when we were young. Just me and her and the tearing wind beneath our feathers, land spilling out below us like a tipped jug of wine, all the doubts and hungers of dirtlife ripped out and abandoned in our wake.

It wasn't just the beauty of the sky that called us. There's a magic to dying things, from the snapped neck of a goose to first love's heartbreak, and a day's no different. Death's as sacred as any bloody birth or sticky act of conception, no matter what priests might say. And the violent prolonged death of the sun spews power into the air like a pyroclastic flow.

We'd get drunk on it, dizzy and over-full with magic. The slow sip of power it took to feed our wings was nothing next to the glut of orange and purple and gold, the hiccuping sweetness of the clouds, the last splash of colour as day succumbed to night.

Sometimes it would take us half the night to make it back up the mountain. Gibbous or crescent, a moon provides no thermals, sheds nothing but dead air and sickly light. We'd beat our muscles to ribbons clawing back up through the sky.

It was worth it.

Worth it for the magic, of course. For me, though, it had always been about those other sticky, stolen moments, huddled close in the crooks of massive lowland ilma trees or tumbled onto the dry pebbled streambeds of the foothills. About laughter and touch and the flitting stroke of feathers.

For Aly, too. Or so I'd thought.

MY PINIONS WERE SINGED.

The smell of ash and burning hair clung stubbornly between the barbs no matter how fast I flew. The ghost sensation of constructed wingbones pulsed threateningly through my magic, sending little fingers of pain through the muscles of my back. The healing incisions ached and tore again, seeping new blood onto old feathers.

That's the price of bonded feathercraft. The sky is yours——but so are all its tiny agonies.

My wings beat. I wasn't the only featherwitch in Breywell Village, and certainly not the only one in the high valley towns that studded the Zephward mountains like sour cherries in a solstice cake. But their wings were knit from snow cock and partridge feather, rounded and multilayered for long, hovering cliff harvests.

I had had a pair like that.

I'd ripped them out my back nine days ago; they couldn't do what was needed. The wings I wore instead were vicious, sharp-tipped things, made for chewing through league after league, and cosmetic charring wouldn't hinder them. They tied deeper into the rings of my spine than any witch would dare to delve, devouring power and oxygen both. My chest burned and burned.

Finally, eventually, I gave in, and touched witchcraft to the bubbling meat of my lungs, coaxing and molding it to fit my needs. It was dangerous, risky magic, as likely to warp flesh as to enhance it. But Aly and I'd paid that price a decade ago, needed it for our long, high flights where the air thinned like milk from an underfed goat. I'd all but forgotten the trick of the thing. The spells we'd built together had hurt too much to use.

If they'd bring me to her now, I'd use every one of them and more, even if it tore my rib cage open to do so.

BY THE TIME I FOUND her, Aly and her crew were hunting once again.

It took me days to track them. Days of hijacking unfamiliar thermals, gliding down unknown trade winds, eking out every fragment of energy I could from storm clouds and starshine and, yes, the angry death of the sun. Days of sleeping hidden in forest canopies, drinking from streams, dodging suspicious lowlanders' arrows like a pheasant flushed from its nest. Days of skirting township walls and fountainmage barriers across a world cut to pieces like goat flesh carved for market.

But I knew how she thought, how she dreamt. And I was hunting, too.

The merchant ship was slow and fat against the setting sun, cargo hanging bulbous as a pelican's pouch beneath the silken carapace of her balloon. This one, at least, had armed herself. Clanking plates of mismatched metals rattled against her hull, the weight dragging awkwardly through the air. Even as I drew close, the flare of cannonfire echoed impotently from her gunports, their sound more like the barking of coyotes than rolling thunder.

They were mudborn, clay-toed ignorants, and they didn't stand a chance.

The Desperante wasn't an airship, not in any sense but the literal. I'd only seen her sketched, before; heard descriptions passed ear-to-mouth through the voices of those who'd never so much as glimpsed a Zephborn trader, let alone a featherwitch. She was both more glorious and more terrible than I had imagined.

Glorious, the way her banks of wings flexed and pulled against the air. Glorious, the bend and weave of her bronze-and-canvas mechanical frame as she swooped around the lead shot and the roaring violence of flamecraft. Glorious, the entirety of her, five times the size of a full-grown drake, feathers brindled brown and gold in the fading sun.

Terrible, the leather-clad featherwitch crew with pistols strung across their chests like garlands, the barely- human rictuses of their faces. Terrible, the crack and cry of birdbone when a wild shot hit home, painful in ways I couldn't fully comprehend.

Terrible, to see the theory and engineering I'd crystallised from Aly's dreams made manifest for this use.

This was my fault as much as hers. I knew her, Alcyone of the West Wind, knew the way her heart burned, the way her temper fractured like splintering bone, knew the damage her kingfisher-swift mind could wreak when the last fragments bent and snapped. We'd grown up close as sisters, then closer still. If anyone could have seen it coming, could have stopped her, it would have been me.

Well.

Better late than never.

THE DESPERANTE. SCOURGE of the Zephward skies, phantom of the Tlelz Abyss, deepest terror of every forgewight merchant clan and sworn enemy of the Alaran Immolate.

It seemed ridiculous. A single feathercraft pirate ship could never materially damage an empire, could never loosen the fire-crafters' stranglehold on the flow of goods, couldn't wrest our mountains free of the Immolate's tariffs and tithes.

But if one existed, then so could more. And that scared them.

It shouldn't. Only two people knew the skeleton of the thing, the siphoning of sun through mountain glass to spin the fragile bones, the force-feeding of energy into eagle and vulture quills until they grew and grew and grew. The gestalt feathercraft you needed to fly the thing. The grotesqueries you fed it to keep it hale.

Only two of us, and neither would teach another. She was too selfish. I was too afraid. The secret of the Desperante's construction would go down with the ship and her captain.

Hopefully very, very soon.

THE DESPERANTE HAD posted no watch behind.

And why should she? I counted no more than a score and a half aboard as I drew closer; she likely couldn't spare them. And the merchant dirigible—the Carillion Ruby, from the gold-flecked paint on her stern—could not possibly hope to circle her.

I was no merchant dirigible.

I looped above her once, twice, learning the pattern of the ship, when she dove and when she retreated. How she moved. I may have designed her, but we'd never built more than models. I'd never seen her fly.

The merchant ship was growing desperate. A cloud bank was forming from the roar of its cannon, acrid and bitter and reminiscent of things I was fighting to forget. Now. I had to act now.

Diving felt like freedom. The wind pushed my cheeks back against my bones, clawed at my goggles, dug into the crevices between my knives and wrenched at my pistols. But I knew its strength. I pulled up before it could tear anything free, soaring forward like a raptor sighting prey, straight for the Desperante's tailfeathers.

They were vulture-like in shape, paler in colour, two times as long as I was tall, and stiff as ironwood. I flared my wings and matched speed, the creak and shout of battle settling across me like a smothering fog. I could hear Aly's voice in the chaos, screaming orders. I knew it instantly, intimately. She sounded so angry.

Gods. How dare she plant doubts and regrets in my heart, when she was the one who—

I dug my nails into my palms until they ached, joining the phantom burn of my wing muscles. The feathers. I was close, now. Close enough to touch.

I stripped off my gloves. Bare flesh is a conduit, any child learns this at the knee of priests or storytellers. The barbs were oily beneath my fingers, smooth and alive and grotesquely large, like insect legs beneath a lens. They twitched and quivered with warmth.

With magic.

I closed my eyes, and drank.

IT IS NOT DRINKING, not truly. Not as plants drink the sun. Flesh is a permeable receptacle for magic; you can glut yourself for hour upon hour and have nothing to show but lingering spasms and the memory of glory.

The trick, then, is to use flesh as a siphon to the soul.

First, you suffuse yourself with witchcraft. Not just the shoulders and rib cage, the spine and neck and back muscles needed to graft the wings, but the whole of you—kneecaps and fingers and the whorls of your feet, the strange pulsing gristle of the engine of you, the fibers that tie bone to bone. Then, at the very moment of repletion, you pause.

Imagine pouring ice wine into a goblet. You can pour until the liquor lies level with the lip of the glass. If you are careful, if the table is steady, the goblet well made, you can even pour a little longer. The wine will cling to itself as it rises, in a curve as subtle as the edge of the world seen from goose-height, above the rim.

You will want the magic to feel like that within you.

Stop. Hold steady. Balance on the precipice of excess, and open the well of your soul.

This is hard to describe.

A priest will teach it as listening to the glory of their goddess. An aesthete hermit will speak of allowing beauty entry. Myself, I think of the wonder of frost patterns blooming over cedar twigs before dawn, when the skies are cloudless and the stars suck all warmth from the trees. You will find your own way, your own key to unlock the frozen quiet awe that lives inside each of us.

Magic calls to magic; wonder to wonder. If you catch the trick of cracking open this door, it will drink eagerly of the sunset or the stormcloud or the stolen crumbs of feathercraft animating your enemy's pirate ship.

It will sip the ice wine from your goblet, and you need not spill a drop.

I SANK THE TEETH OF my will into the witchcraft beneath my fingers, and I ripped.

Metal groaned. Feather tore. Magic gushed away into the air. The hollow shafts of the quills I touched collapsed in on themselves like stream-banks swept away in a storm. The desert dregs of my reservoirs swelled under the deluge. I flapped harder, fighting to stay abreast of the tailfeathers as the Desperante yawed above me, unable to hold steady with half her tail falling away like ash in the wind.

The tone of the shouting had changed. Less bloodlust, more fear. Featherwitches came tumbling up from the ship's canvas like glassfoxes out a smoked burrow, their wings barely unfurled as they jumped. Fragile, makeshift things, fashioned for short bursts of extreme agility——they'd not catch me.

"Lady Alcyone!" came the shout from above, from the open-topped platform where the ship's wingbones socketed themselves to brass. "Lady, they're getting away!"

The pirate was right. The Desperante could barely hold a steady elevation, let alone give chase, and the Carillion Ruby was making for the horizon as fast as her propellers could spin. I felt a grim spark of triumph kindle in the back of my throat, and doubled my effort as the last great rectrix crumbled away to dust.

From above came a terrible, high-pitched noise of fury, the cry of a hawk deprived of prey. As I fell back, the Desperante wallowing in the air, Aly appeared above me like a vengeful god.

She'd barely changed. Gods, with the sky behind her and her wings outstretched, it was like time itself had fallen away around us. She stole my breath.

And then I folded my wings and dropped, sluggish and stupid as a fledge, as she dove towards me cutlass-first.

Slow, I was too slow—her blade caught my shoulder, tore across. Blood danced in the wind. My bandolier fell, spiraling away beneath us. I clamped one hand across the wound and wrenched back, boosting my wings with the magical remnants of the Desperante's tailfeathers.

"Have I changed that much?" I didn't mean to say it, let alone boost my voice to slip it into her ears above the rush of the wind and the laboured clank of the Desperante.

But there was joy to this, to seeing her again, bubbling alongside the rage and utter resentment I'd been nursing for days—no, years—if I tore away the scab, forced my guilt into the light. Years of watching the mysterious coin and silk and linen, the forgecraft and foreign seeds, as they appeared in the houses of families who'd misplaced a young witch or two. Years of suspicion and gnawing anxiety every time the Immolate's officers tallied us at midsummer, at midwinter, wondering if this would be the time someone slipped. The time they noticed.

No. She wasn't my Aly anymore. I was facing Alcyone, Pirate Queen of the West.

But my voice had stopped her.

"Kes?" she said, like a little girl, baffled and uncertain. Her wings beat, swiveling in place, leaving her bobbing in the air, and I realised she had changed. She'd adapted her wings. They were as long, and still primarily vulture-feathered, as the ones I now wore, but the joints were different, the musculature tweaked. Optimised for a different style of flight.

Of course they were different. Alcyone of the West Wind didn't need to fly for leagues with nothing but travel bread and the strength of her back—she had her ship for that.

I turned into the wind, letting it pin me in place. "Yeah," I said, throat sore. Had I spoken at all since I fled the ashes of Breywell? "It's me."

"You—you nest-wrecking piece of crowbait, do you know how long that's gonna take to repair?!" Nose crooked and proud like a shrike's beak, cheekbones and brows and chin like the edges of cliffs gone round only grudgingly with age, hair shorn tight and curly against her scalp; her voice was high and taut with fury.

"A real long fucking time," I said, feeling my face crack open in a grin, and flicked my knives up out of their sheaths.

She had the upwind advantage and was unwounded, but I'd been preparing for this ever since the first lick of flame touched timber. I'd known exactly who I'd been facing.

I closed with her before she could draw her cutlass back into a guard, my wings more powerful than hers—I was half again her weight and stronger by far. She'd cut away my pistols but knives were more satisfying in the thick of it, more intimate. The heat of her gasp seared against my ear when I rammed the first blade home.

"Gods-dammit, Kes, why—get off!" The blade was too short, a tool more than a weapon. I'd barely pierced muscle beneath her leathers. I tried to wrench it back, bring my other knife around, but the first had snagged inside her armour and she'd grabbed my wrist before I could get the second in close.

We strained, legs tangled, wings beating, bobbing gracelessly through the sky like ducks swept over a waterfall. "You know why," I said, my knife pushing closer, and closer still. "You've known."

"Why—why now," she panted, bewildered. Vulnerable.

A trap.

She'd dropped the cutlass. Her hand was free. I realised it a second too late as the poison of her witchcraft stole into my secondaries, unraveling them where they lay.

With a shout, I let go of my knife in her vest and shoved.

We broke apart. Miles downwind of the foundering Desperante, hundreds of yards lower—I couldn't see the billowing smoke of the Carillion Ruby at all anymore.

She was laughing. My knife still jammed into her ribs to its hilt, black blood slicking her leathers, and she was laughing.

"Kes, Kes," she said, voice cruel with affection. "You never learn."

I jammed my knife back in my belt, reached around behind me. I was listing. She'd destroyed feathers on the same side she'd sliced my shoulder. The arm was already stiffening. I could knit the cartilage together again, but it would take time. Time with land beneath my feet.

But she was wrong. I did learn. I patched the baldness in with pure magic, spun barbs from the brimming well within me. It would hold for now, but it was not strong or subtle. I wouldn't be able to turn as fast, dive as sharp. I wouldn't dodge her again.

"You can't fight me," she was saying, certain as a child. "You won't fight me. I'll never believe you'll finish it." She had drawn a dirk from her belt while I fixed my wings, and now she caressed it, wight-forged steel shining like glacial ice. "So why don't you tell your Aly why you're really here?"

"To kill you," I said, hand going to the hilt of my knife.

"Steady," she said, pistol appearing suddenly from her belt, its silver barrel pointed square at my chest. "Let's not be hasty. Why, love? You want my riches? My crew? My ship?" She flew closer. I held still. "You know I'd kill to have you by my side. It's only your stubbornness—"

"Never." My voice was shaking. "I'm here to burn all that to the ground." Her dirk was almost gentle where she rested it against my breast. "Like the Immolate did Breywell."

She flinched. Just for an instant, but I saw it. Horror. Guilt. Denial. "They did what? When!"

"A tenday ago." A little more. It had been late morning. They'd come at dawn.

"I'll kill them," she said, eyes hard like flint, dirk gone loose in her hand. "By Vymis's teeth, I'll kill them all—how many? The young ones, the elders—did they escape?"

"They let us go." Gave us two fingers of the sun to gather food and tools and the infirm, to huddle under blankets in the cold morning light as we watched them burn our homes. I'd been beyond lucky to find these wings intact in their chest. "None dead."

It had been close. Mylz had almost thrown a punch when they'd refused to let him rescue his little one's cradle. Nilta had thrown a curse—she'd survived only because the agents hadn't known enough to recognize it and because she'd missed. "It was a warning."

"A warning?"

"We featherwitches are to stop our raiding. Or they'll return."

Her eyes narrowed. "Ah," she said, soft as a snow owl's wingbeat. "I see. And so you come to kill me."

"And so," I agreed.

"You're wrong," she said. "They won't leave you alone if you hand them my head."

"Maybe so."

"They strangle us day after day. We die a little every time we bow. Kes, how can you ask me to live like that? How can you ask it of any of us?"

"I don't."

She was expecting me to fight, I think. Expecting to retread the same familiar arguments we had woven again and again, blistering the air between us in those last months before—before she'd left me.

"I'm not a child, Aly," I said, slowly brushing her blade aside. "Just because a boulder allows the river to flow over it doesn't mean it can't eventually turn its path. And you haven't the saltpetere or the sulphur you would need to blow its banks. You're just an annoyance to them. A bad storm could take down as many ships as you do."

"Oh, shut up, Kes." She laughed. It was a wet, bitter sound. "You always were a pompous ass."

She let me move the knife, slipped it back into its sheath. She pressed the pistol to my heart instead. "I can't just do nothing. I won't. I never will."

"And I can't let you keep doing this." I couldn't. At any moment, the Immolate might decide we had gone too far, that feathercraft was toxic, the Zephward lands untameable. Anathema, like the fategilders and their crystal ruins, drawn out by superstitious envy and slaughtered by song. They would drive us from our homes and into the highest ice valleys, into our caves and mines. Into hiding. Into extinction.

The Desperante was just the excuse they needed.

"Stalemate," Aly said, and the click of her pistol was almost swallowed by the wind. "Oh, wait. No, it isn't."

But I knew her. I'd known her. Her focus was sharp as obsidian. And yet she was here, with me, instead of up above, wrestling her beloved ship into working order, rescuing her tumbling crew.

She wouldn't believe I'd kill her. She couldn't. And until she did, she'd never bring herself to kill me first.

She still loved me.

Could I kill her, knowing that?

Did I have a choice?

"Perhaps," I said, instead softening my voice, my shoulders, the tilt of my wings. I had never been good at dissembling, as a girl. The years had taught me much. "But you don't want to shoot, really. Do you?"

I reached out. We were close, now—I didn't need to stretch. My fingers were resting on her skin. My smallest blade nestled half-forgotten in its wrist sheath.

Soft. So soft, for such a harsh face. I rubbed a thumb along her cheekbone. Slid it down past her ear, felt the fluttering of her pulse. She bit her lip. Said nothing.

My wings beat. Hers, too. They fell into a rhythm. Drew us close, closer still, until the toes of her boots nudged against my shins. The barrel of her pistol pressed hard against my ribs.

I kissed her.

I shocked her, I think. I used to think I never would. But she hung there, lips slack, chapped from the wind.

She didn't taste of blood. Just chill skin, perhaps the scent of gunpowder, of grease. Her lips moved against mine. She began to raise her hand.

And I tore the bottom out of the well of her magic.

I hadn't known I was going to. Hadn't known it even to be possible. But if flesh is a conduit, and wonder a reservoir, then in the press and yield of lips, I discovered a further truth: love is the gateway, the sundering of self, against which all walls crumble.

Through the channel of our devotion, I stole it all—her craft, her knowledge, her years of hoarded power like a wyrm hissing in the darkest deepest caverns of the mountains. And rather than swallowing it, I destroyed it.

What else could I do? It was not enough to take. She could rebuild. Out of spite, out of hatred, she would rebuild, and turn her rage on those who had harmed her: the Immolate, who had despoiled her childhood, who ruined her people. And me.

So I reached, desperate and ignorant and filled with prayer, down the avenues and vessels of her power, and every path I traced I sealed behind me.

She screamed. I barely noticed—the magic burned like I was the one destroyed—even though her lips left mine, and her hands clawed at me like an animal, slipping away, pistol forgotten in her panic. Her wings disintegrated around us, feathers tumbling like debris from a kestrel's kill, and she tipped back out my grasp, arms wheeling. Falling.

No. No, it couldn't end like this. It couldn't. I'd found a way—a way to win, a way to end her piracy, a way to save us from her short-sighted fury, a way where my quick-witted, jewel-bright Alcyone could survive. Seething, wounded, hating me with every shred of her soul—but alive.

Love, I discovered, was a weapon which cut its wielder just as deeply as its target.

I folded my war wings like sleek daggers behind me, twisted in the air, and dove.

Jennifer Mace is a queer Brit who roams the wilds of the Pacific Northwest in search of tea and interesting plant life. She writes about strange magic and the cracks that form in society. Her work is forthcoming in Enter the Void and Cast of Wonders; find her on Twitter as @englishmace.

The Birthday Heist

by Fred Yost

CAIUS'S EYELIDS STARTED to droop near the end of his first hour locked in the brig. Goddamned lulling motion of the goddamned airship.

Should've been easy money. Save some people while collecting a nice bounty. That's how Ma'd sold the job to him. Couldn't blame her though. He'd fucked up, got snatched up by the first security patrol he'd run into after they stowed away on board. Splitting up had been a good idea. The rest of the team had avoided capture. At least, none of the rest were in the brig. Safe on board, or wounded in the sick bay, or killed and tossed over the side. Helluva way to kick off his birthday.

"Got any coffee?" Caius asked the guard, a faunus named Halloway.

Halloway shook his head. "Wouldn't waste it on you if I did, werewolf. Zach says the Sapphire Order's gonna kill you as soon as we reach port."

Caius blinked. "What? Why?"

"Zach said they'd kill you. That's all I know."

Motherfucker.

"Shit. Got anything stronger than coffee?"

Halloway pulled a flask from his pocket. "Yeah. But..."

118

"But why waste it on a dead man."

"I'm sorry." Halloway looked back as he set the flask on his desk. "I...can't."

Caius leaned against the cell wall. So much for decency. "Fuck you, too, buddy."

He tried to ignore the sudden wave of nausea rising inside him. Hell of a time to get motion sick, or have some weird reaction to the silver in his cuffs. He took a measured breath, practicing a deep-breathing technique Rei'd shown him. Calming shit. Break the situation into digestible chunks. He just needed to escape, find Pru, get her to break him out of these goddamned manacles unnoticed, lure away one of the heavily armed elite guards, knock them out, steal their armor, shift, not lose control, and take out all seven wizards before any one of them could cast the spells to kill almost everyone on board for some dumbass ritual. Easy fucking peasy.

But first he needed his stomach to settle. He'd close his eyes, just for a second.

Caius sank into darkness. Fire. Blood and blades. Blue-robed figures dragging eldritch creatures from crystalline prisons with bloodstained ropes. Death heaped upon death.

He rolled to his knees, dry heaving. Visions were Rei's department. If he was seeing something like that, he knew for sure those damned mountains were the real deal, and the ship was too goddamned close. He spit a mouthful of what he hoped was blood.

"You okay in there?" Halloway asked.

Caius tilted his head. Something felt different in the air. Under the unpleasant scents of the brig, a new smell floated through the air ducts. Distant. Cucumbers with a hint of musk. Either Miche'd been nabbed or escape moved towards him.

He turned back to Halloway, surprised to see genuine concern on his face. "Like you care. If you cared about anyone, you wouldn't be working for those murderers."

Halloway moved closer to the cell. "What do you mean, murderers? If you hadn't stowed away... It's harsh, but it's not technically murder. I'm sorry."

Caius idly tugged at the bars. "You don't get it, do you, kid? Would have been a helluva lot easier for me to hit the ship and grab the wizards on the way out, when it was almost empty, but that'd be a lot of folks dead when I could have stopped it. Ritual sacrifices to elder demons ain't my jam."

"What the fuck are you talking about?"

"Like you really don't know? Don't bother bullshitting a dead man."

"I signed on two weeks ago. They put up a posting and hired a bunch of us, amazing pay. Too good to ask questions. And they made me a lieutenant right off the bat."

Caius leaned against the bars. "Never could figure how a death cult got an experienced crew to work for them. They didn't, did they?"

"Post said they wanted fresh folks. Ones without bad habits they'd need to train out."

Caius rubbed the bridge of his nose. "That didn't set off some alarm bells?"

Halloway looked to the ground. "I needed the work."

"Must have. This whole trip is full of red flags. None of the passengers look like the type to go on a luxury cruise. Damned few'd notice if they went missing. Fewer still would care."

Halloway took a shaky sip from the flask. Caius heard the click of a lock somewhere down the hall.

"I'm dead, you're dead, life sucks. Sure you can't spare a drink?"

"Promise you won't eat me?"

"For fuck's sake," Caius said. He faintly heard mumbled words from the other room. A countdown in a sibilant tongue. Not much time at all. "I don't fucking eat anything I can hold a conversation with."

Halloway stumbled to the cell. Caius smelled the whiskey on his breath. A fuzzy hand reached through the cell bars. The countdown stopped. Caius grabbed Halloway's wrist and pulled hard.

"Do me a favor and don't scream."

Halloway screamed.

With a sigh, Caius bent the faunus's arm at an uncomfortable angle so he could cover Halloway's mouth without letting go of his wrist.

"Seriously, kid, I don't want to hurt you, but you gotta keep quiet and cooperate."

Halloway quieted.

The door slid open, revealing a vaguely feminine silhouette. The smell of snakeskin intensified.

"Salutations, Bosswolf," the newcomer said.

"Hey, Miche. Kid here has the keys."

Her flats tapped lightly on the metal floor as she moved closer, licking her lips. The dim light revealed a forked tongue dancing over bright white fangs.

"Venison? You spoil me."

Halloway yelped into Caius's palm. Caius slammed the faunus's head against the bars.

"Quiet. Miche, just the keys, please."

Miche grumbled, but he heard the jingle of keys freed from a pocket. Halloway mumbled something into Caius's hand. Caius relaxed his grip.

"Largest key opens the cells," Halloway said.

"And the shackles?" Miche asked.

"No keyhole," Caius said. "Should've tipped me off they never intended to open them."

The door popped open. Caius maneuvered Halloway into the cell as he stepped out.

"Good job, kid, almost done. Hold tight in there, and before you know it, we'll either let you out someplace safe or you'll be dead."

"You said you weren't going to hurt me," Halloway whimpered.

"We won't, but if we can't stop the blue robes in time..."

"Bosswolf, time comes. Mountains grow near. Demons hunger."

Caius slid the cell door shut and followed Miche through the rectangle of dim light at the end of the brig. He broke into a steady jog as soon as his eyes adjusted to the hall's lights.

"How long was I locked up?"

"Too long. Paired hours? Maybe more."

"Shit. I should have figured a way out sooner. Or at all. Wait. Why did you come get me? Are they out of wine already?"

Miche glared. "Wine was boring. Everyone else, occupied. Needed you out."

"Everyone is in place on the observation deck?"

"Blue robes? Yes. Civilians? Yes. Our crew? Technically."

"Technically?"

"The Lady grows anxious."

"Best not to keep her waiting." Caius lifted his cuffs. "Speaking of easing her anxieties, anything you can do about these?"

"Bosswolf."

"What?"

"Did not magically cure rage virus in lockup, yes? Without Lady's ice, you will lose self to blood."

"I won't shift. I just...I don't like being trapped like this."

"Poor Bosswolf, trapped as mere mortal."

"Please."

Miche grabbed his wrists and muttered a few arcane words. She pulled back with a hiss.

"Alarms. Traps. No time to bypass."

"Alarms? Do they know you magicked them?"

"Not likely, but possible."

Caius picked up speed. They still had half a ship to cover.

"Halt!" called a gravelly voice as he rounded a corner.

Caius slid to a stop, bracing for Miche to slam into his back, but her tongue had always been better than his nose. Rock golems, even those in woolen guard uniforms, didn't smell like much.

"Evening, good sir," Caius said. "Is there something I can do for you?"

The mottled guard lifted his blaster and pointed it in Caius's general direction. "Could pretend ya don't think I'm an idiot?"

"Beg your pardon?"

"You're the werewolf that was in the brig," the guard said, slurring. "I remember the shirt. Distinctive."

"My fucking shirt? Really?"

The guard belched, then chuckled. "All right, the silver bracelets helped."

Caius glanced at his wrists. The manacles definitely gave him that "*escaped prisoner*" look. "Don't suppose you'll let me go so I can save everyone's lives?"

The guard blearily studied Caius. "Not likely. Gonna take you back to your cell and punch you until you tell me how you got out. After that? We'll play it by ear."

Caius felt the hair on his arms stand on end as red pulsed in his vision. Calming breaths. He couldn't transform. The silver protected him. The virus couldn't take hold unless he transformed, right? "Maybe you go upstairs, have a drink, and relax."

"Fuck no," the guard said with another belch. "Awful party. Took forever to nick a little wine. S'okay though. Shit's strong. Now get moving so we can make with the hitting."

Caius took a deep breath. "Do they pay you enough for this? You saw the bounty. The rumor is they're going to kill me. I must be dangerous."

The guard shrugged. "Danger's literally in the job description. Interrogating you is a fringe benefit."

Caius heard the light tap of flats moving down the side hallway. "Hate to disappoint, but you don't need to hit me. I'll tell you how I got out."

"Oh?"

Miche stepped from around the corner and grabbed the guard by the back of his neck, pressing a small cylinder to his temple.

"I had help," Caius said.

"Drop your weapon," Miche said. "Kick to Bosswolf."

The guard hesitated.

Miche licked the side of his neck and grinned at Caius. "Maybe inside taste like rock candy?"

Caius met the guard's wide eyes. "I wouldn't test her."

The guard did as she asked. Caius turned the blaster on him. "This thing have a stun setting?"

The guard glared.

Caius clicked the safety off. "C'mon, buddy. Keep cooperating."

Miche ran her hand over the guard's arm. "Near four hundred pounds, yes? Mostly muscle, some rock?"

The guard glanced at the blaster. "Three fifty. Mostly muscle. Rock skin's lighter than people think."

Miche twisted the tube a quarter turn. "Wise to answer. Improper dosage could be dangerous."

"What?!"

The tube sprayed a puff of powder in the guard's face. He blinked twice, dropped to his knees, then toppled forward.

Caius frowned. "Dead?"

Miche shook her head. "Unconscious."

"Useful that. Something of theirs?"

"Not quite. Made a new toy."

"When?"

Miche shifted her weight, not meeting his eyes. "Told you. Dosing wine was boring. Made something to react with our additive. Right dose means unconscious enemy."

"And the wrong dose?"

She pocketed the tube. "Important to get right dose."

Caius didn't ask how she found that out. He turned his attention to the fallen golem, who'd stood just over five feet tall. "Think you could do that with a guard closer to my height?"

"Guards know each other." Miche tapped his wrists. "And you stand out."

"True."

"Waiter?"

"They're dressed like goddamned sailors. How would that stand out any less?"

"Too obvious to be noticed. All they see is waiter."

Caius sighed. "That makes sense."

"Will take a moment to procure. Better to take time than get caught."

"Just be quick about it, please."

Miche led Caius past the observation deck to a side room and told him to wait. He paced. Every second of delay meant more danger.

Just stay calm. Time for more fancy breathing. Think about clear skies and happy things. Think about birthday dinner.

As he took another deep breath, the faint sounds of giggling and the sharp smell of arousal interrupted his thoughts. Miche stumbled into the room, arm in arm with a tall, bulky, human man. The man froze when he saw Caius.

"What's going on?" he asked. "I thought—"

Caius tried not to notice the man's pants were unzipped. "Look, I know you're a bit dazed right now, so I'll take this slow. Bad news is you're not getting laid right now."

Miche glared.

"Good news is it's my birthday, so if you cooperate, I won't hurt you."

The waiter looked at him, obviously confused, but able to focus without effort.

"Fuck. You didn't drink any wine, did you?"

"Can't. Allergic to grapes."

"No shit, really?"

"Ever since I was a kid. Ended up in the hospital at my first communion."

"Hmm," Caius said. "Do the blue bastards pay you enough to get concussed for this gig?"

"No." The waiter rapidly shook his head. "Do you have any idea what kind of long-term damage a concussion can cause?"

Caius leaned against the door. "Fair point. My scaled associate is going to take your clothes and tie you up. Don't make a scene and don't attract the attention of a guard and we should be fine."

Caius could only describe the look on the man's face as a mix of fear and anticipation. "Yeah, I'll do it. Whatever she says."

Miche leaned close to the waiter. Caius turned his attention out the viewport. Clothes slowly landed at his feet. He struggled to change while manacled. Pants, he could manage. Shoes, too. Soon, all that was left in the pile was a pressed shirt and...

"Hey, uh, I don't need his underwear."

"Not everything is about your needs, Bosswolf."

Caius tapped his wrists together, carefully keeping his gaze on Miche's face. "Magic up a shirt switch for me, please."

Miche distractedly waved her free hand and Caius's shirt peeled off his body in strips. A hissing chant sent the waiter's puffy white shirt crawling up Caius's torso, sliding in place over his manacles.

"Go now. Am not needed for fighting."

Caius fought off a sigh. He hated to begrudge anyone their simple pleasures, but now was not the time for distractions. Or leaving the most volatile member of his team alone. "Of course we need you. You're our problem solver."

She let out an exasperated sigh. "Why do I listen to you?"

"I'm your boss and our secret base has a sweet lab?"

"No. Could eat you, become new boss, take lab."

"Because you're a wonderfully talented magical potions ninja and it's my birthday?"

Miche rolled her eyes. She looked back at the naked waiter and then glared at Caius. "Fine, but do not blame me if I accidentally eat someone. And you, naked man. Give me your number. We'll finish this later."

Caius tapped his foot impatiently while waiting for Miche to jot down the waiter's info. They had time, he kept telling himself. They'd be cutting it close, but by the gods they'd still have time, even if he had to will it into existence.

Outside the observation deck, he grabbed a hand towel off a nearby table and used it to cover his wrists before stepping into the room.

The sight of the crowd poked at something in his heart. Every goddamned one of them in their threadbare Sunday best.

Except for two assholes in Hawaiian shirts. Otherlanders of all kinds, the only unifying factor that they all looked tired and hungry, and except for a few huddled families, lonely. Reminded Caius of the foster families he'd bounced between before he fell in with the O'Sheas. With Mairead. Ma. He hadn't told her, but he'd have taken this job even without the payout for the wizards. But first, he had to do the job.

Easy to spot his crew: Brayden standing near the plexiglass window, talking up a storm; Rei at the DJ booth, headphones around her neck, dancing to music not yet playing; Alex, hovering by the door marked PRIVATE, ready to slip onto the flight deck and hot-wire the airship's auto-pilot.

Easy to spot the wizards in the blue robes, scattered throughout the room. Same for the seven-foot-tall, steel-plated elite guards watching over them.

Not easy to spot Pru.

She couldn't afford to be seen with a bunch of thieves, so she'd come aboard in disguise. But he damn well knew what that disguise looked like and she wasn't anywhere he could see. Her smell lingered throughout the room, fire and ice and metal and flesh. Everywhere and nowhere, a bit of olfactory camouflage born of Miche's boredom on the East Bay job. Great when they needed her hidden from other shifters. Not so great when they needed to find her.

Except she'd left her body armor back at their apartment. So why metal? Unless...

"Fuck."

Miche raised an eyebrow.

"She already took out an elite, didn't she?"

Miche shrugged. "Not before I leave to get you. But she had concerns about time."

Caius grumbled as he studied the room. So much for Pru not getting involved with an easy job. "Double fuck. Blues're too far apart."

"Almost as if worried about attack from one person?"

Caius growled softly. Focus on the targets, find a solution. He smiled. Each one carried a mostly empty champagne flute. He tapped the tube in Miche's pocket. "Think you could take out the Order of Murderous Fuckery if I make a big enough distraction?"

Miche surveyed the room. "Very big distraction, perhaps."

Caius whistled three short notes, barely audible over the ambient noise of the room. Brayden searched the crowd, his eyes widening momentarily when he spotted Caius. Caius nodded.

"Distinguished guests!" Brayden's voice cut through the hushed conversations around the room. Melodic. Powerful. "If you take a look out the observation window right now, you'll see we're approaching the Lightspire Mountains, quite possibly the oldest known formations in the entire Otherlands, according to this hastily constructed pamphlet they handed out as we boarded."

All seven blue-robed figures and all but two guards turned towards Brayden. Miche took a step back into the press of the crowd, blending in almost instantly. Caius grabbed a nearby tray of wine glasses and maneuvered to the nearest inattentive guard. He took a deep breath and fought off a flinch. Ogre skin and ball sweat. Definitely not Pru.

"What the brochure doesn't tell you," Brayden continued, "is the Lightspires are home to Soultaker Ridge, the site of numerous sacrifices attempting to unleash an ancient evil."

The murmurs took on an unsettled edge. The blue robes exchanged confused looks. Without Miche's additive in the drinks, there might have been a full-blown panic.

Caius sidled up to the other guard. This one, at least, smelled of nothing that might keep her from being Pru.

"Wine?" he asked, doing his best to disguise his voice, just in case.

The guard backpedaled away, drawing a large falchion as she moved. "Escape!" the guard cried. "The werewolf's escaped!"

"Shit." Caius allowed that perhaps his British accent wasn't as good as he thought.

Caius moved to the center of the room, studying the rest of the guards as they approached, trying not to let anyone get a clean shot at his back for any length of time. One of the elites didn't move a smoothly as the others. Caius could see their breath in the air, despite the heat from the bodies filling the room.

Of course. She couldn't fit in the giant suit of armor without some kind of filler, and ice drew a helluva lot less attention that lava.

He charged the armored figure with the frosted breath, his arms stretched over his head. The guard grabbed the chain between the shackles and lifted him high in the air.

Motherfucker. Wrong again? Pru'd give him so much shit for not being able to find her. Assuming they survived, of course, which... Well, odds weren't great, now that he'd been grabbed again. Hell, he already felt the creeping chill of death.

Wait, no. Not death. Just regular cold seeping into his arms through the manacles. Caius grinned.

"Hi, darlin'," he said. "Ready to cause a distraction?"

"'Bout damn time." Pru's voice, unmistakably hers, echoed in the large suit of armor.

She dropped him. Heavy boots pounded on the ground far behind him. She swung her hammer down and he caught the blow with the frosted silver manacles. The shockwave from the impact reverberated through the room as the hammer exploded and pain blossomed in his side.

Caius blinked as silver shards rained down around him. Why would his side hurt?

He looked down to see the blade of a falchion protruding from the ruffles of the shirt he'd stolen from the waiter, blood pouring from a gaping wound. Ow. His own bitter laugh rang in his ears. Sonnuva bitch. On his birthday no less.

"No!" Pru shouted.

The air went dry as the ambient moisture turned to flurries of snow. Frost cracked along the edges of her armor, branding the steel. Pru punched the falchion wielder hard enough to send the guard flying into a wall.

Caius staggered forward, the bitter laugh turning into a chuckle. Heat poured through his body, radiating from the cut. A steel blade. Not enchanted. Not silvered. Just plain fucking steel. He shook the last silver shards from his shaggy hair. Nothing keeping him from shifting now.

The heat turned to burning. The chuckle turned to a howl. Heart pounding. Vision narrowed to blood-red pools. A clawed hand ripped the blade free from a furry side. Flesh knitting as the falchion pulled free. Thoughts of torn throats, shredded armor, and a feast of blood and ogrekin flesh.

A metal gauntlet gripping a furry arm. A flood of cold magic pouring through the arm. No. Him. His arm. His heartbeat slowed. The red faded from his vision. One of the elite's dangled limply from his claws. He could taste blood on his canine teeth. Shit shit shit. He tossed the guard in Rei's general direction, hoping she'd be able to keep them alive.

"You okay, fuzzbutt?" Pru asked.

Caius nodded, not trusting himself to speak. Pru lifted her arm from his and formed a blue-and-white longsword in her hand. They stood back to back. The remaining five elites circled them slowly, less confident now the odds were a bit more even. Caius glanced at the wizards, worried they might take matters into their own hands, but only three remained standing. Two stared raptly out the window, no doubt counting down the time before one of them could start the ritual. The third watched the fight, hands waving in the air. Before Caius could say anything, Miche appeared next to the waving wizard, a tube at her lips. Then only two remained.

A blade slashing past his face brought his attention back to the fight in front of him. Pru caught the sword in her free hand. A blast of frost shot from her gauntlet and engulfed the weapon. The elite pulled back and struck again. The blade shattered on Pru's armor. The answering swing of her sword sent her opponent flying to the ceiling, the icy shards of their weapon pinning them in place.

Caius stepped up to another, dodging an ax swing. He fought with no fancy magic, nor practiced form, only a flurry of claws and teeth shredding armor, but that served well enough. He stared at the guard's throat. One bite could end it. Deep breath. A single punch knocked out the exposed ogrekin.

He looked up to see Pru slamming one guard into a wall. The elite collapsed and didn't get back up. One left. Caius checked the room. He looked up in time to see the last wizard open their mouth to begin the ritual, but Miche stepped up beside them. A single puff of powder sent them sprawling to the ground.

The last elite tossed their weapon to the ground and dropped to their knees. Caius picked up the oversize cutlass and planted his foot on their chest.

"You surrender?" he growled.

The downed fighter choked out a desperate chuckle. "Fuck yes, I surrender. The shit I've seen, man, I did not sign up for. And those assholes do not pay me enough to die for them."

Caius started to let the guard up, but Pru signaled he should wait.

"Fellow travelers," Brayden said, his voice reverberating beyond the acoustics of the room. "All unpleasantness is out of the way. Please calm down."

The crowd immediately settled. Brayden was a damned good siren.

"Please think of this as a rescue mission. We'll be taking a detour to the Lightbringer mountains, a real tourist destination. Emergency services will undoubtedly provide you passage home."

Trusting the drugged wine and Brayden's spells to keep the passengers calm for the remainder of the journey, Caius turned to Pru.

"Can I let this guy up?"

"Not yet," she said. "Miche?"

Caius turned to the click of a camera. Pru pulled a sailor's cap from the suit of armor and placed it on his head. Caius flushed.

"Just go with it," she whispered.

He struck a pose that wouldn't have been out of place on the logo of a rum bottle, a silly grin creeping on his face.

"Should I send Rei to the sick bay for an eyepatch?"

Caius coughed. "Not necessary."

"A little ice parrot?"

Caius pointed the sword in Miche's direction. "We done?"

"You're the bosswolf, Bosswolf."

Caius tossed the sword to Pru. She grabbed it midair and pulled the ogrekin guard to his feet. "You seriously repent getting involved with these killers?"

"Of course. Everything about them was horrific."

"Then come with me," Pru said. "Let's talk about your redemption arc."

THE SMALL OFFICE IN the hangar indirectly owned by the O'Shea Syndicate lacked any sign of a personal touch. But it served well enough as a front, if you didn't look too close.

Prudence shook flecks of ice from her shirt while waiting for the prisoners to be pulled from the brig. Nephilim didn't need to worry about cold, but if her top got too wet she'd need to go back to the apartment to change. And she'd already told Caius she'd deliver the wizards so he could have time to make himself look less like he belonged on the cover of a particular brand of romance novel.

She watched a stately older woman walk down the gangplank of her airship.

"Evening, Ma," Prudence said.

"Lady Danakil, I do not care how close to the boy you are, if your mother heard you call me Caius's little nickname, I'd be in as much trouble as if she found out you accompanied those ruffians on their jobs," the woman said. "Please. Call me Mairead, or Ms. O'Shea if ye must be formal."

"Fine, Mairead, but you need to call me Prudence. Or Pru. I'm no Lady Danakil. Not here."

"Of course, dear," Mairead said, thumbing through a stack of papers.

"I trust you found everything in order?"

"Seven wizards, neatly bound. Seven matching bounties posted by the Danakil Corporation in the last hour. Big bounties. Big rewards."

"Then we're square?"

"More than square. Your debt's paid on the bounties alone, even after cutting Caius and his crew their share. Add in the airship—"

"Apologies for any confusion, the airship is mine now. Just coincidence that happened to be the best way to apprehend them."

"Bullshit. Coincidence, dear? Just like it was coincidence a concerned guard called in a tip the same day your love took this job?"

Pru stretched. "Lucky break, that."

Mairead clicked her tongue. "Lucky? Don't lie to me. Lie to Caius, if you must. Using insider information never sat well with the proud idiot."

"Danakil's enforcement division has been trying to get the Order of the Sapphire Revenant for years. Too long. But it only made it to my desk last week."

"So why today? The fools haven't succeeded in summoning an elder god yet."

"I didn't want anyone to die while waiting for a bureaucrat to authorize a strike. And if I'm being honest, the timing was too good to pass up."

"Timing?"

"Don't tell me you've forgotten Caius's birthday. He'll be heartbroken."

Mairead rolled her eyes. "You've got the best table in Ship-wrecks, with dinner from a chef I flew in just for tonight. What does his birthday have to do with the fucking job?"

"Two months ago, they picked up that guard thing on the East Bay. I tagged along. Easy money. Boring job. We talked. About the past, our dreams, and some silly things." Prudence tucked her hair behind her small horns. "Caius told me he'd always wanted to be a pirate."

She showed Mairead on of the photos Miche'd taken.

Mairead smiled. "I see. Get on out of here and give the birthday boy my best."

"Of course." Prudence paused by the door. "You can borrow my airship for now, but take good care of it. The worlds may need the Dread Pirate Caius to fly again."

Fred Yost is a writer, gamer, and pet owner. During the day he works tech and at night he stalks the shadows of Central Texas to howl at the moon. Wait, no, I mean when he's not writing or playing video games, he's probably rolling a character for some RPG or another.

Airships are Overrated (Always Insist on Taking the Kittens and Puppies Valley Route)

by Laura Davy

EVELYN HAD ALWAYS THOUGHT an airship would be grand and awe-inspiring. With a gleaming deck, masts reaching the clouds, and sails glimmering with magic. Instead it was a box.

No deck, no portholes, no rails, and not even a hint of a sail. Just a wooden bottom with four short walls.

Definitely a box.

Sure, the magic to make a ship fly could be used on any object. But airbox didn't have the same ring as airship.

A stranger who seemed more beard than man walked over and smiled at the structure with a manic gleam in his brown eyes. "Stargazer's a beauty, isn't she?"

Evelyn glanced around to see if he was talking to her. Or maybe talking about a different secret ship hidden away. Though from the way he looked at the box this object had to have some redeeming quality. Perhaps she didn't know enough about air travel and the square design made it extra safe.

He slapped the side of the box, making the structure shudder as if it was on the verge of collapse.

So, not safe then.

The man asked, "Are you interested in booking a ride?"

Evelyn glanced skeptically at what was probably a deathtrap, but it wasn't like she had many options. It would take her a month to walk to school and it would cost too much to rent a stagecoach.

"How much does it cost to go to Aveility City?"

"Aveility, eh?" He stroked his beard and looked at her, taking in her youth, secondhand robe, and the fact that her visible luggage was ninety percent books and ten percent tea. "Isn't that where the wizard schools are? You know we offer a discount for wizards if they don't mind helping out a bit."

Evelyn quickly decided he didn't need to know this would be her first year at school and so she wasn't actually a wizard yet.

"What's the discount?" Evelyn asked, hoping she didn't sound too interested.

"Half price if you just help power up the flight spell every now and then."

"Deal."

"Good. Name's Conor and I'll be the one flying you and anyone else who wants to go. Now let's figure out what route we should take." Conor pulled a large map out of nowhere. Either he knew magic himself or the map had been hidden in his beard. "Company doesn't send us enough wizards to fly everywhere we want, but Aveility is important enough that you have a few route options. Different stops along the way, but they all land at the city."

"Is there a difference in price?"

"For you? No." He stretched out the hand-drawn map and pointed to the different colored lines, clearly routes or someone was really bad at drawing country boundaries. "Let's see, you could take the Red Route, takes you across the Boiling Lake and the Give-Up-All-Hope Mountain. That's the quickest way and you'd reach Aveility in six hours."

"Boiling Lake and Give-Up-All-Hope Mountain," Evelyn repeated. "Isn't that dangerous?"

"Oh, I wouldn't think so."

Evelyn eyed the skull and crossbones so cluttered on the map they left little room for landmarks. "What are the other options?"

"The Yellow Route takes you over Valley of the Tortured Souls and Forest of the Damned."

"Pleasant."

"Though for the best view I'd recommend the Blue Route over Annihilation Peak, Eternal Rest Mountain, and the Cliff of Ruin. Basically over the entire Death Mountain Range."

Who came up with these names?

"Couldn't I go over the Kittens and Puppies Valley or something?" Evelyn asked.

"Oh, God, do you have a death wish?!? Though speaking of death wishes, the Green Route over Death Wish Valley would get you there in two days."

"What's the safest route?"

"Umm..." Conor avoided meeting her eyes. "They're all safe."

Evelyn glanced over at the airbox/airship. The less time she had to spend in it the better. "I guess the fastest route."

EVELYN VOWED NEVER to take the fastest route again. And never ride an airship again.

The wind stung her eyes and it was so cold even layering on two of her winter coats didn't help. The box was crowded with at least a dozen passengers sitting side-by-side on the airbox's floor, most of whom looked either bored or terrified – which were the two feelings Evelyn herself fluctuated between.

And then there was the nausea.

None of her books mentioned feeling ill while flying. Then again all of the books claimed airships were valid transportation options so nothing the authors wrote could be trusted anymore. Conor claimed Evelyn was feeling seasick, but how could she feel something that happened on the ocean when they were flying through the air? Evelyn would have pointed out the logical problem, if she wasn't afraid of what would happen if she opened her mouth.

At least the scenery was beautiful. Forests reduced to patchwork greens, snow-peaked mountains, and turquoise rivers cutting through it all. Give-Up-All-Hope Mountain really should be a vacation spot.

"Hey, wizard." Conor's voice cut through Evelyn's thoughts. He sat upfront, which really was just the side of the box facing the direction they were headed, with his hands on a steering wheel, which was really just a stick. "Add some magic to the seal, would ya?"

Evelyn placed her hand on the magical seal that kept them all airborne. The spell looked like a small hand. Each time she refilled the magic it felt like that hand reached out and punched her in the gut. That probably didn't help with the nausea.

"How do you fly this thing without a wizard onboard?" Evelyn asked, looking at the other passengers and wondering just how long they'd had to wait before a flight.

"We don't. But at least once a week some wizard wants a ride, or we temporarily hire one, then we fly. Worse comes to worse, we get one drunk enough to pass out and then wake them up about halfway in. At that point they have to power up the spell."

Kidnapping confession aside, Evelyn wondered if she could have gotten a better deal than half off. And the fact that not a single passenger seemed surprised by the unorthodox methods simply confirmed that anyone willing to fly was either foolish or fearless.

"You know," Conor continued, "If schooling doesn't work out we could always use wizards around here. Travel, adventure, and maybe a little windburn, all yours for the taking."

Evelyn vowed she'd never leave school.

"By the way, what happens if there's a storm or a dragon finds us?"

"Dragons usually don't bother ships, something about us being beneath their dignity or whatnot. And our airships are made to handle even the toughest storms. But neither of those are usually the issue. What's the problem is pirates."

"Pirates?" Evelyn repeated with an added amount of skepticism. "But we're in the sky, how could pirates reach us?"

Now if pirates were to suddenly appear right after Evelyn asked the question, she would know never to tempt fate again. But naturally that didn't happen. Events don't occur just be-

cause someone spoke out loud. No, the pirates came ten minutes later.

"Incoming off the starboard side!" Conor yelled out,
pointing to the right.

Two small figures were speeding towards the airbox.
Squinting, Evelyn could make out two people balancing on
what looked like flying boards. Literal boards. A plank of wood
that they balanced on without even a railing.

Did no one understand the concept of the "ship" in airship?

The two pirates zoomed closer and a voice that was so loud
it had to have been enchanted by magic called out, "Stop flying
and surrender!"

"Never!" Conor yelled out with such passion that Evelyn
didn't have the heart to tell him there was no way the pirates
would be able to hear him at such a distance without magic.

But given that the airbox wasn't slowing down, the pirates
appeared to have figured out they weren't giving up. And with
that, the pirates started throwing spears and the passengers
started to scream.

This wasn't good.

"Quick," Conor yelled to Evelyn as a spear with a rope tied
around it just missed the airbox's side. "Power up that seal!
We've had a lot of missing ships from this route so the pirates probably don't leave survivors. Our only hope is to outrun
them!"

Evelyn slapped her hand against the magic seal and added
power to it, realizing it didn't make her feel nearly as sick as the
fear did.

"Do you know any attack or defense spells?" Conor asked as he made them soar even higher.

"No! I haven't even taken a single class!"

"Should have guessed you were new when you settled for working for just half off rather than money and a free ride."

Evelyn quickly noted never to make that mistake again. Well, if she lived through this and could make more mistakes.

Another spear flew above them, barely missing Conor's head.

"We outnumber them," Evelyn shouted to Conor and the cowering passengers. "Maybe we could beat them in a fight."

"They have magic and weapons, what do we have?"

One of the passengers stood up and threw off his cloak. He was armed with more weapons than a standard army and it looked like even his muscles had muscles.

"Don't worry," he declared as the wind tussled his hair. "I will protect you!"

A spear hit him in the head.

The would-be hero collapsed into a heap. As the other passengers screamed and cried - which seemed like a smart action given the circumstances - Evelyn crawled over and checked out the body.

The man groaned and clutched the spear attached to his head. Literally attached. It was a rounded spearhead with no point, but it must have had some magical spell to make it stick to whatever it hit. Plus there was a rope tied to the spear. But why?

As if to answer the question, the rope went taut. The man slid towards the side of the airbox, as if someone was trying to reel him in.

Evelyn looked out at the pirates and saw they were moving hand-over-hand on the rope to close the distance between them and the airbox. Attached by rope, now even the best ship maneuvers wouldn't be able to lose them now. The pirates would be on them in a matter of seconds if this continued.

Evelyn grabbed a knife from the unconscious man's belt and sawed off the rope. Maybe that would make the pirates fall. Evelyn gazed out, hoping to see nothing but sky. Instead, the pirates were getting closer.

She really should have insisted on traveling the route across the Kittens and Puppies Valley.

"What's happening back there?" Conor called out.

"Nothing good!"

"Are you sure you don't know any spells?"

"I only know small spells, like warming up tea, finding lost sheep, and making my voice louder," Evelyn trailed off and then looked back at the pirates. "Actually, should we try negotiating?"

"Didn't you hear me?" Conor asked as the airbox dived down, making Evelyn remember why she had felt nauseous for most of the flight. "A lot of airships don't return from this route. These pirates don't just take your money. They take your life."

"It doesn't hurt to ask."

Ignoring Conor's shouts of protest, Evelyn cast the spell to amplify her voice. Then, as another spear passed over her head, she called out, "Will you stop chasing us?

Well, at least it was worth asking.

"No," a pirate countered with a voice also magically louder. "Surrender!"

"No. We don't want to die!"

"Who said anything about dying? We wouldn't kill anyone! Rough them up a bit, sure, but not kill!"

The confusion in the voice was only amplified with how loud it was. Either the pirates were terrific actors or they really weren't murders.

"But we heard you don't leave survivors," Evelyn said with a meaningful look at Conor.

"That's just bad for business. Too many deaths mean people wouldn't fly here anymore, and then we'd have no one to steal from."

"Plus, killing is like, super bad," the other pirate called out with a magically enhanced voice. If they both had enchanted voices, that means they both could use magic. "We'll steal, but we draw the line at murder."

Great, two wizard pirates and Evelyn could only magically make tea hotter. At least it looked like they weren't going to kill them all. Maybe.

"But airships have been disappearing on this route," Evelyn said.

"That's probably from the dragons and storms. Very dangerous."

Evelyn sent another meaningful look at Conor, who studiously ignored her. They continued flying as quickly as they could. The wind was giving Evelyn a headache. And she still felt sick.

"Could we all just stop and talk this out?" Evelyn cried out.

"A parlay?" Conor and the pirates asked at the same time.

"Sure," Evelyn replied. Whatever a parlay was, it had to be better than this chase.

The airbox slowed down and the pirates slowed down as well. They were clearly experienced with flying since they wore multiple jackets, a number of scarves, and goggles. Oh yes, and at least a dozen gleaming weapons each looking scarier than the last.

Soon everyone simply hovered in the sky and glared at each other. Off to a good start.

"Well," Evelyn said slowly as she rubbed her temples. "If storms and dragons are so dangerous then why would you risk flying yourselves?"

"Not a lot of ways to make money here. A few years back, we changed the area's name to Hope Mountain in the hopes of becoming a popular vacation spot, but somehow the name changed to Give-Up-All-Hope Mountain."

Evelyn considered the name apt given the dragons, storms, and pirates, but wisely didn't comment.

The other pirate spoke up. "We even went to a wizarding school so we could learn a new trade and were kicked out before the end of the year! Apparently they didn't like it when you prefer fighting to reading. We don't really want to be pirates, but we need to make money somehow."

Good thing schools didn't teach lightning attack spells until the second year.

But even if the pirates didn't know attack spells, they were already so powerful. The spears, the speed, and the ability to balance on a board over a thousand feet off the ground and not freeze in terror. They had to be either fearless or foolish to be a pirate. Just like everyone else who liked airships.

"So," Evelyn said as an idea began to form, "would you be willing to relocate if you could make money?"

The two huddled together and silently chatted before one called out, "Sure. I mean, as long as we could visit home every once in awhile."

"And could you endure travel, adventure, and maybe a little windburn?"

"For money? Sounds like a dream!"

Evelyn looked towards Conor. He laughed and said, "I think I know where you're going with this, little wizard. And I like it! Always preferred fighting over reading myself."

With a smile Evelyn turned back to the pirates. "Have you ever considered becoming airship pilots?"

After that it was just down to negotiations.

THE ONCE-PIRATES AND now-pilots left with company employment contracts and only a few stolen coins. They even healed the would-be hero's concussion without being asked.

Conor turned to Evelyn. "Don't worry, the rest of the route should be just as easy. Probably. Maybe. With luck it will be just as easy!"

Evelyn vowed that next time she'd just walk.

"AIRSHIPS ARE OVERRATED (Always Insist on Taking the Kittens and Puppies Valley Route)" © 2018 by Laura Davy

Laura Davy wrote her first story when she was in elementary school, and despite the fact that the plot didn't make sense, she kept on writing. She's been published in Apex Magazine, Escape

Pod, Grimdark Magazine, Grievous Angel, and others. Find her at www.lauradavy.com or @TheLauraDavy on Twitter.

Runaway

by Joshua Curtis Kidd

"NO ONE ESCAPES THE Guild," Jacob Shelley said to himself as he chased a rebel up the side of a mountain. He hoped that he wouldn't allow the first exception today.

Jacob aimed the three-pronged claw of his sparking iron at a tree just beyond the rebel. He summoned his magical energy, and a bolt of electricity arced between his sparker and the tree. Its bark exploded in large chunks.

That ought to have been enough to convince the rebel to lay down her rifle and return quietly to the munitions factory with him. Instead, she turned and fired her rifle at Jacob.

His shield stone stopped the bullet in an explosion of blue light. Jacob stumbled, disoriented by the flash, and the rebel continued her run for the woods.

Jacob could have caught her already, if he had used his flash stone. He held back because he wanted her to give up and realize the futility of running from The Guild. His orders were to capture or kill. He wasn't ready to kill.

The rebels were idiots, persisting in a war that had ended more than a hundred years earlier when King George III had hired The Guild to crush their forces. They were an underground group now, and their methods included assassinating leaders and blowing up buildings. They no longer even had a clear cause. Queen Victoria ruled the American colonies in name only, and The Guild was paid by an American government to keep the peace.

Keeping the peace sometimes meant meeting the rebels with lethal force. Jacob knew that such things were required to maintain the greater good, but it was a different thing to have to do them yourself.

The rebel turned to fire at Jacob again. Two other Guild members flashed up beside her. The hoods of their robes hid their faces. Lightning leaped from the ends of their sparkers at the rebel. Jacob turned away, but his shield shimmered blue as dust and heat pelted it.

No one escaped The Guild.

Jacob returned to the munitions factory, which was now engulfed in a magical green flame that would consume bricks, iron, steel, and everything else. Soon, only a pile of smoking ash would remain to show that any structure had ever been there.

Nestled in a valley in western Virginia, this factory had escaped the notice of The Guild for some time because the rebels hadn't constructed it along a major river. It ran on steam power, and nearby mines provided the coal it needed for fuel.

Jacob found his mentor, Benjamin, overseeing the building's destruction.

"We might never have found this place if we hadn't tracked that airship making a delivery of iron," Benjamin said. From up close, his long gray beard and sharp cheekbones were visible under his hood." They might have continued to manufacture rifles here for years. We're saving a lot of lives here today."

Jacob nodded. This was for the greater good.

"I heard that the rebel that I sent you after was dealt with," Benjamin said to Jacob. His voice and expression were full of disappointment. Benjamin knew who had dealt with the rebel.

"That's right," Jacob said.

"I need you to handle something else for me," Benjamin said.

"What is it, sir?" Jacob asked.

"A few rebels escaped into the woods this way," Benjamin said. "There should be three of them. I need you to find them and deal with them."

"I understand," Jacob said. Benjamin was testing him, seeing how far he would go. He was giving Jacob another chance.

"I knew I could count on you," Benjamin said and put a hand on Jacob's shoulder.

Jacob had seen how The Guild dealt with failure. He still didn't know if he could summon his magic to kill another person, and he was afraid. He touched his belt and flashed into the forest.

The range of travel with a flash stone was a few hundred yards under normal conditions. In the forest, the density of trees shortened that range to only fifty yards or so. Jacob could use the stone to open temporary portals for quick travel, but only to locations within line of sight. He would have to progress more slowly here than he could out in the open, moving back and forth across the forest in an expanding pattern.

With each step through a portal, complete silence engulfed Jacob. On the other side, sound returned just as abruptly.

Jacob emerged from the silence to a man's scream, and he saw a figure dive behind a large boulder. In fear, Jacob's magical energy surged forward and out through his sparking iron. The rock exploded, and pieces flew in all directions.

It was getting dark, and the electric arc of the sparking iron had blinded Jacob. He stepped past what remained of the rock, squinting to see. Jacob hoped that the man was dead. He had fired without thinking much about it. He wasn't sure he could fire on the rebel again if he had to.

Jacob found the man lying face down, hunched over something else. He was bleeding from several wounds where he had been struck by flying rock fragments, and he was no longer breathing. Jacob rolled him onto his back.

Beneath the man, Jacob found two other bodies. They were children, and they were also dead.

Jacob raged at the man's stupidity. He had not only run from The Guild, he had put his children in danger by taking them as well. Magic surged up within him and again he fired his sparker. The bolt struck a nearby tree, splitting it in two. The sudden destruction startled Jacob out of his rage, and guilt came forward to take its place.

He had been a fool to think that he could remain a part of The Guild and avoid complicity in its brutality. He had been trying to escape The Guild while still remaining a part of it. And Benjamin had sent him here, knowing that Jacob would have to murder children.

Jacob couldn't go back to the factory. He couldn't escape, but he had no other choice. He had to run. He touched his belt and flashed away.

JACOB FLASHED THROUGH the evening without stopping to eat or sleep. He found the North Star in the sky and he followed it. When morning came, he stopped to learn his location from some people he passed, but he refused to rest or look for food. Hunger and exhaustion soon caught up with him.

When he arrived at his mother's boardinghouse in his home town of French Creek, Jacob felt like he was dreaming. His mother came out to welcome him home with tears in her eyes.

He had had many dreams like this since joining The Guild. He always woke from these dreams, lying on his cot in The Guild dormitory, knowing that his dreams were showing him something he wanted to be real.

His mother had been so angry when he left. She had told him that if he left for The Guild, then he wasn't any son of hers. He hoped that one day he would come back and show his mother all of the magic that he had learned and tell her of all the places he had been. She would understand why he had left French Creek to join The Guild, and she would forgive him.

When Jacob woke in a soft bed rather than a Guild cot, he knew that his memories of the night before had been real. The room was the one he had grown up in. The quilt on the bed was one that his mother had made with fabric stitched together to show birds flying through the clouds.

Jacob's limbs were heavy, but he pulled himself up from the bed. His robes and everything he was carrying the night before were piled in the corner. He heard his mother talking beyond the door and went to find her.

"Mom," Jacob said, but his voice was weak.

From the top of the stairs, Jacob could see his mother talking to a man who put on his coat and left the house.

"Mom," Jacob said again and nearly stumbled down the stairs.

Eva Shelley ran to her son's side to support him. "I've got you," she said. "You shouldn't be out of bed yet."

Jacob was surprised to see that he was taller than her now and that she had streaks of gray in her hair.

"Who was that, Mom?" Jacob asked.

"It was just a boarder," Eva said. "I've sent him away. It's just us in the house now." She put her shoulder under her son's arm and led him back to bed.

"I'm going to go out to get us something to eat for tonight," Eva said. "But I need to know something first, Jacob. Are you back?"

"I don't understand, Mom," Jacob said. "You can see that I'm here."

"No," Eva said. "I mean have you left The Guild?"

Jacob had to think about the question for a moment before he could answer. "Yes," he said at last. "Yes, I have."

Eva smiled and hugged her son. Jacob could see tears welling up in her eyes. "I thought I'd lost you forever," she said.

"I'm surprised you would take me back," Jacob said.

"I never felt as bad as when you told me you were leaving to join The Guild," Eva said. "And things haven't gotten much better in the five years since then. If you're back, then maybe that can change. They say forgiveness is a virtue, but I'm just ready to not feel so terrible anymore. We can talk more about it later. You should try to get some more sleep."

Eva left the room, but Jacob couldn't fall asleep again. Saying aloud that he had left The Guild started something stirring in his mind.

He couldn't really have left The Guild. No one left The Guild, just like no one escaped The Guild. He might have run away, but they would come for him and they would kill him. And, if he was with his mother when they came, they would kill her, too.

Jacob got up and extinguished every lamp in the house. He grabbed his sparker and waited by the front door, watching through a window the dirt road that led into town.

When Eva returned home, Jacob pulled her into the house.

"Jacob," she said. "You should be in bed."

"Mom, I think I may have put you in danger," Jacob said.

"I know," Eva said. "The grocer said that some men from out of town were asking about you."

"Then we need to leave now."

A bright flash of light outside interrupted them.

Jacob used the iron-claw muzzle of his sparker to move the curtain on the window just enough to see the silhouettes of two robed figures.

"Come on," he said. "We have to go out the back."

Jacob couldn't see anyone behind the house, but The Guild wouldn't give them an easy escape. He removed the chain that held his shield stone and put it around his mother's neck.

"When we go out, run for the woods," he said. "We might be able to lose them in there."

Eva nodded and remained quiet.

Jacob pushed the door open slowly, taking two careful steps. A bolt of electricity struck the ground in front of him, sending up a spray of dirt and smoke.

"Run, Mom!" Jacob shouted. He still couldn't see the Guild member, but he fired his own sparker in the direction from which the shot had come. He hit a tree, igniting a few dry autumn leaves that still clung to the branches.

Jacob fired a few more shots and then flashed into the woods, catching up with Eva in the cover of the trees.

"I need to tell you something," Eva said.

"No, Mom," Jacob said. "We have to keep moving."

"Keep moving where?" Eva asked. "I appreciate your willingness to act quickly, but we also need a plan if we're going to escape. We need to get to the airship docks."

"What good will that do us?"

"I never told you this, but your father and I were part of an airship crew before you were born. When you came back last night, I reached out to some old friends—"

"Mom, we can't outrun The Guild. Not even in an airship. They're going to catch us, one way or another."

"Jacob, I'm trying to tell you that the ship was our home, one that we took with us wherever we went. We weren't always safe, but it was our bubble of freedom in a world controlled by The Guild."

"Maybe it would be better for us to split up," Jacob said. The Guild was after him and not his mother. But if they found the two of them together, Eva's fate wouldn't be any different than his. "You can go to the airship docks, and I can go draw them off."

"Jacob, that's not what I—"

The rest of Eva's words were cut off when Jacob flashed deeper into the woods.

JACOB STEPPED THROUGH a portal onto an empty baseball field. Eva was still in the woods, and he needed to draw The Guild's attention.

He fired his sparking iron at the wooden bleachers, which exploded into a hail of flaming splinters. The remaining boards continued to burn, illuminating the field with a flickering light. The Guild would see where he was, and he would see them coming. That was what he wanted.

A flash of light just beyond home plate drew Jacob's attention, and three hooded figures emerged from the shadows. Each carried a sparking iron trained on him.

"I don't expect mercy," Jacob said. "But you should expect a fight."

"And why wouldn't you expect mercy, Jacob?" Benjamin pulled back his hood to reveal his face. "Your mission was successful, and you haven't done anything wrong yet. Do you think that you're the first of our initiates to question his commitment to The Guild?"

Jacob had expected The Guild to send men he didn't know, men who could kill him without hesitation. Benjamin's even voice disarmed him.

"I know what happens to members who try to leave The Guild," Jacob shouted.

"It's true," Benjamin said. "We can't let anyone leave with our secrets. But I'm giving you the chance to tell me that you're not leaving. That you had a strong reaction to a bad situation and that was all."

"A bad situation? You sent me to kill children," Jacob said.

"I didn't know that there were children," Benjamin said as he walked slowly toward Jacob. "If I had, I wouldn't have sent you. Not without help and without a plan to bring them back alive. That factory was producing more than fifty rifles a day. Think of all of the lives we've saved by destroying it. We work for the greater good, Jacob. You know that."

"I shouldn't have been sent to kill anyone," Jacob said. "They just wanted to get away."

"Jacob, I truly regret the decision I made," Benjamin said, putting his hand on Jacob's sparker. "And I would rather no one else die for my mistake. Let's go back to the Guild Hall in London and discuss this. We don't need any more violence."

Jacob wanted to make another argument, but that wouldn't be the end of it. Making arguments was just like running. He could do it until he was exhausted, and The Guild would keep coming.

Jacob let go of his sparker in resignation. "All right," he said. "I'll go."

"Excellent," Benjamin said. "We'll get a portal set up to transport the two of us to London immediately."

One of the Guild members behind Benjamin pulled a keystone from his pack and set it on the ground. The other waved his hands over it and began muttering incantations.

"You're making the right decision, Jacob," Benjamin said. "When we get back to London, you'll feel—"

Benjamin's words were cut off by the sound of an engine starting above them. An airship was circling overhead to land in the field.

"Quickly, now," Benjamin said, pulling Jacob towards the keystone where the shimmering mist of a portal was forming. The keystone could open a portal to any other keystone in the world, but it required more time to work than the flash stones.

"We're losing the connection with London, sir," one of the Guild members shouted.

"It's the airship," Benjamin shouted. "Fire on it."

The Guild members pointed their sparking irons towards the ship, but nothing happened. Rifle fire sounded from the direction of the airship, and one of the Guild members dropped his sparker to grab his arm. The mist above the stone was dissipating.

"Our sparking irons and shield stones aren't working, sir," shouted the Guild member who was hit. "Neither are our flash stones."

"All right," Benjamin shouted. "Back into the forest. Don't leave that sparking iron behind. Jacob, come with me."

Jacob stood still, transfixed by the sudden appearance of the airship.

Large sails protruded like ears from either side of the cigar-shaped gas envelope. Two long poles extended from each side of the gondola, and at the end of each pole, a spinning propeller pointed skyward, pushing the ship down toward the field for a landing. But why had The Guild's magic started to fail as soon as the ship appeared?

Jacob remembered what his mother had told him. The airship was her bubble of freedom in a world controlled by The Guild.

"No," Jacob said. "I've left The Guild, Benjamin. I'm not going with you."

"I'm sorry, Jacob," Benjamin said. "I can't let you stay."

Jacob felt a sharp pain in his abdomen and looked down to see a knife's hilt and a growing blood stain on his shirt.

"I'm truly sorry, Jacob," Benjamin said.

Jacob fell back onto the grass and lost consciousness.

WHEN JACOB WOKE, HE lay in bed. Eva sat in a chair beside him, holding his hand. Little else could fit in the room besides the two pieces of furniture, and Jacob thought he could feel a gentle swaying.

He tried to sit up, but his mother put a hand on his shoulder.

"Easy now," Eva said. "You almost died. It's a good thing for all of us that Dr. Plowright was aboard."

"Where am I?" Jacob asked.

"This is Windchaser," his mother said. "You were born on this ship, you know. I suppose it might have been poetic if you had died on it as well, but I've never much cared for poetry myself."

"Mom, what happened that night?" Jacob asked. "Why weren't The Guild members able to work their magic?"

"Well, The Guild likes to shroud themselves in an air of mystery with their silly robes and complicated rituals, but their magic is really just another kind of technology. It can be studied and understood. And we've been studying it for decades now. The engineer on this ship came up with a machine he thought could disable magic at a short distance. He was eager to try it out, and Captain Merriwether owed me a favor."

"How?"

"That's what I was trying to tell you that night. I've been a part of The Resistance for your entire life. After you were born, I had to leave this airship for a life that I thought would be safer, but I continued my work. The boarding house was a way station for Resistance members passing through. I'm sorry that I didn't tell you when you were younger, but the wrong word to the wrong person could have gotten us both killed. Then you were off to join The Guild, and there was nothing I could do."

Jacob had to look away from his mother. How could she be part of the rebels? Had some of her boarders been assassins? Had they blown up government buildings? He had wanted out of The Guild, but joining the rebels didn't sound much better to him.

"Mom, have you ever killed anyone?" Jacob asked.

"I haven't," Eva said. "We all resist in our own way. But I won't claim that I don't know plenty of people in The Resistance who have killed. And that includes some of the people on this airship."

"So, I've left The Guild only to join the rebels?" Jacob asked. "Why can't I just find a place to live in peace?"

"Because peace in this world is the order maintained by The Guild," Eva said. "Anyone who threatens The Guild's power to maintain order is dealt with violently, and they call it peace.

You can't peaceably separate yourself from The Guild. To do so is to be part of The Resistance."

Jacob was too weak to think through his mother's words, but a phrase bubbled up through his consciousness.

"No one escapes The Guild," Jacob said.

"That's right," Eva said. "No one. But if enough of us get together, maybe we can escape together."

All of those years, his mother had been part of The Resistance, and The Guild hadn't taken them. Jacob hadn't done nearly so well on his own. He might not ever escape The Guild, but he could run much farther with help.

"I don't know if that's true," Jacob said. "But I'm willing to find out."

Joshua Curtis Kidd has lived in Boston, Atlanta, and Los Angeles. He currently calls Philadelphia home. When not reading and writing, he spends his time taming the magical beast saccharomyces cerevisiae. You can find him online at www.joshuacurtiskidd.com or on Twitter at @joshcurtiskidd.

Clockwork & Consensus

by Mary Alexandra Agner

IFIGENIA GLASS ADJUSTED the tiller and watched dawn come up through the clouds. She pulled her cloak tighter around her shoulders, but it wasn't the altitude that chilled her.

By now the wizard Ransaransa had probably noticed she'd escaped. The wizard would probably be tasting the wind, working out Ifigenia's direction and speed, debating which monster to command from the menagerie. Ifi flinched at the thought of claws closing around her.

She consulted the hypsometer and the azimuth-rose. She would make the floating city of Seffel by nightfall if the weather held. If the air currents didn't pull her off course into a cloud lagoon rife with sky sirens, who preyed on humans. If she avoided the pirates known to infest these skies. If she could stay awake to steer. If, if.

She had a contact in Seffel willing to sell her clockwork for a small cut, both her prototype worker and her airship. She ran her fingers slowly along the railing of the captain's hut. Her heart and sweat were in its copper and pine finish; already it was difficult to let it go. At least she was still tinkering with the autonomous clockworker.

The light level dropped. Ifi stepped onto the bow of the ship. Between her and the sun were two pirates, keeping time. Larger craft than hers, probably holding half a dozen people each, more than enough to take her and her ship.

She winced, imagining crushing grips and harsh voices. Her pistols? She'd meant them for intimidation. They'd do little against the metal hulls of the ships, but they could deter the pirates themselves—if she could bring herself to use them. Panic jerked from her chest to her limbs like a coil spring released.

"Ehoy! Little craft! What have you got to pay our tax?" The speaker leaned over the deck of the closer pirate. Brown hair cropped short yet rising and falling with the wind, brown skin nearly the color of his hair. "I am Obrahom of the Cirrus Circle, and we claim this current."

"Ridiculous," Ifi muttered under her breath.

"Do you think so?" Obrahom asked, laughing. He gestured with his hand, and the wind between them fell still.

In the silence, Ifi heard singing, a long chord held by multiple voices and then released. She could make out a handful of people now standing on the deck of each of the pirate ships.

Encouraged by their small hands and Obrahom's cultured voice, Ifi repeated herself, louder. "No one owns the air."

Obrahom nodded. "Certainly, the air is its own. But we all have desires. And we all have to eat. The design of your ship is unique, so small a craft, run by a single person. We want the details. Schematics? You look like that type. Let us rummage about in your hold, and we'll let you go."

Ifi thought of her unfinished clockworker, of having to kick or punch the pirates or fire her pistols. "No."

Obrahom shrugged. "Thisle?"

A woman with blond braids leaned over the railing. Then she and Obrahom began to sing, and the others joined in, no words Ifi knew, but her vocabulary was full of cranks and gears and tolerances and the many ways people said five and ten and zero. Not magic. Definitely not magic.

While they stayed at a distance, it was easy for Ifi to envy the way the pirates worked together. She understood harmonic oscillations better than harmonies but could read their body language: they received and listened and passed on like a water clock spilling liquid from one jar into another.

At one point a few of them linked hands, and Ifi shuddered. She recalled Ransaransa and other mages slashing their palms and clasping together bloody fingers to make a circle, how it was the last wizard standing who gained the others' power, how the static electricity raised Ransaransa's hair and clothes when the wizard turned to Ifi and made demands. Ifi had tried to make her insides as stiff and resilient as those of her clockworkers, but her heart had always skipped a gear tooth. She never wanted to make anyone feel that way. She had measured the amplitude of impending violence in the width of the wizard's smile, the diameter of the wizard's pupils.

The threat in the pirate's voice earlier was nothing like that. The pirates' song now was like oscillating clock pendulums of different lengths, surging in volume and congruence of pitch when the long rods swung in synchronicity. It felt magical but nothing like Ransaransa's magic.

Ifi shook off the thick memories as ropes descended from the pirates' ships and began to loop themselves into knots around her ship's railing. The first few missed––the music swelled––then grappled successfully, tightening.

Thisle, Obrahom, and another woman levitated over the side of the ship to land on Ifi's deck while they sang. The second woman was taller than the others, her skin less sun-kissed and more night-sky-dark.

Ifi turned to run, tripped over the side of the captain's hut, and threw her hands out in front of her to break her fall. She landed on her front, the pistols in her pantaloon pockets digging into her thighs.

As the music ended, Obrahom stepped over Ifi and grabbed her wrists.

She jerked away, but the other women stepped closer.

"Now," Obrahom said, pulling her upright and passing her wrists off like a parcel, "why don't you stay here a moment with Thisle while I look in your hold?"

Thisle began to hum. Ifi struggled in her grasp; Thisle's grip didn't shift. The second woman picked out a little harmony against Thisle's tune. But she made a face each time Thisle increased the pressure on Ifi's wrists, which Ifi appreciated.

Their music did nothing to cover the sounds of the other pirate on the ladder, then boxes and bins being shifted and metal levers being used to pick open Ifi's cargo. Her mouth was as dry as pig iron in a puddling furnace. Would he lift up the tarps?

"Ah! What a beauty!" Obrahom's voice.

Listening hard for the shifting of her tarps, Ifi instead heard more singing, multiple voices, intricate harmonies, like interlocking gears supporting and winding each other. Crisp and cold, like the air about her, and most distinct from the pirates' song.

Ifi tore away harder, and Thisle let her go. Her muscles felt like lead, squishy and heavy. Thisle stood still, head cocked, listening. The second woman stood still, too, listening.

A quick glance up showed her nothing, but Ifi tugged two grease rags from her belt and mashed them into her ears. She pushed herself through the muffled quiet toward the ladder, descended. Her special crate was safe in the corner, still disguised by paint-splattered tarps.

Obrahom was slumped next to the crate of weather balloons, his hands full of pry bar.

She felt bodies hit the deck above her. Sirens alighting? Humans dropping unconscious? She crawled to the crate of weather balloons, then looked back over her shoulder toward the ladder.

Rainbows fell through the hold. Ifi shivered, recalling that the patagia of sirens were magically-bound droplets of water. Jointed digits, longer than a human's, grasped the top rung, the lower rung, then suddenly disappeared. Ifi could imagine the shrieks, some so high no human could hear them, according to a professor at Kuntun University.

Her eyes on the ladder, she reached into the crate and felt for a switch. Off to on. Second switch. Off to on. She could feel the metal vibrating, the crate vibrating. Off to on. Her weather balloons––silver, spherical, propellers spinning, lighter-than-air gasbags hefting them upwards––rose over her head, seeking the current.

Ifi climbed up to peek onto the deck. A cacophony of color blinded her, overlapping rainbows projected onto the ship, its gasbag, even her own skin. Enormous wings filled the air as the sirens swooped and dove, trying to outmaneuver the balloons. The flight of the sirens was the strongest local current so the balloons followed them.

She laughed at the sight, so hard that a rag fell from her ear. She clapped a hand to her head. In that brief moment of movement, she heard piercing clicks, not song.

She stuffed the rag back into her ear and climbed onto the deck. A siren swooped low over her head, its long canines yellowed and dull compared to the rainbows. Ifi fell to the deck to avoid the bits of sharp bone veining between its wing membranes.

As she watched, it banked and headed back for her. She scrabbled for her pistols. Could she fire at a living being?

The siren dove, opening its snout to aim its call at her; Ifi felt herself pinned to the deck––except her heartbeat, which seemed to be pounding through her sternum.

The siren banked and began to descend toward her body. When she felt her hands shaking, she asked herself again, could she fire at a living being? She'd put herself back together after the wizard's beatings; she'd escaped the wizard's fortress. She would do what she had to to survive.

Ifi bit her lip––then raised her arms and squeezed the pistol's trigger. The siren dropped––Ifi saw blue sky through its torn wing––and Ifi's heart dropped. The siren struggled to rise over the ship's railing, then fell again. The rest of the flock plunged afterward.

Ifi was as empty as the pistol's chamber. Her hands continued shaking even after she rolled over to pin them to the deck. She had hurt someone, she had bloodied them intentionally. Was she any different than the wizard? The flexing of the deck and the ship's balloon against the airstream gave her no answer.

Slowly Ifi sat up, pulled the rags from her ears, pocketed them, and went to check on Thisle and the other woman. Pulses pounding but sleeping. She tied their wrists together behind them, but gently. Down in the hold, she did the same to Obrahom.

She counted the remaining weather balloons. More uses than she'd realized. If only she didn't have to climb down into the hold to turn them on. She hefted the spent pistol in her hand. She scrunched up her face as she thought. The pirates could be useful if she could manipulate them rather than fight. Ransaransa might still find her.

She picked out a sunny spot on the deck to convert her pistol into a device for calling the weather balloons. She breathed in the cold push of the wind, absent when she was trapped in the wizard's fortress.

She'd had to leave behind every flying being in the wizard's menagerie, their cages all locked by blood and magic. The carrier pigeons with their iridescent plumage and enormous tail feathers, whom she'd befriended to secretly transport her letters in and out with Ransaransa's mail. The mega-bees, soft like kittens and as playful, who'd kept her company with their antics. The red dragon, most fearsome of Ransaransa's prisoners until you got to know them, their insistence on bright yellow cheese for snacks, their love of pranks, the low note in their throat when they indicated to Ifi they were thinking of home.

The glint off her tools woke her from a nap. The sun had moved past its zenith. Ifi looked about frantically, but the pirates were still sleeping.

No. One of the pirates on the far ship stood. Ifi grabbed her remaining pistol and shot into the air.

"Wait!" A woman's face looked down over the railing. "Can we just talk?"

"Speech but no song. I had a remedy for the sirens, I've got one for you, too." Ifi looked pointedly at the pistol in hope of confusing them. She hadn't managed to finish the control device. What other leverage did she have?

The woman paled. "Of course." She called out loudly, "Ekren! Wake up! You've got to open negotiations with the clockmistress." And insufficiently softer, "Because I'm not going down there."

The dark woman struggled to sit up with her hands tied behind her. She smiled broadly at Ifi once she was upright. "Hello, fair clockmistress! Perhaps we started on the wrong foot." Ekren's grin was infectious. "Yes, see, wrong foot." She raised one leg into the air, nearly overbalancing herself.

Ifi heard pirates from the other ships laughing. "Ey!" Ekren called, "Wrong foot!" And suddenly Ifi saw pirate feet sticking over the railings of their ships. She couldn't help it, she burst out laughing.

"You are terrible pirates." Ifi curbed her laughter. "And I don't mean that in a fearsome or efficient way."

"Well, we're new at this sort of thing." Ekren's smiled dimmed. "It's not our long-term career choice. It's just been the best way to enable our traveling. We've been making our way to Seffel because, well, you see, in Rijk––"

"Your home?"

"Mine, yes, but not Obrahom's or Thisle's. They come from somewhere further west. And Seht and Nenet--" Ekren tilted her head up and behind at the woman Ifi had spoken with earlier--"they're from Kuntun. But we're a family, you see, that's how we make magic. And--"

"No one approves?" Ifi was startled by the sympathy in her own voice; she'd been holding on to it so tightly.

Ekren smiled. "Yes."

"Not in Rijk nor Kuntun nor somewhere further west," Ifi said quietly, not really a question. Ekren nodded. "I had thought everyone, well, liked magic?" Ransaransa's many rants on the importance of magic began to unspool through her memory, longer and louder and with more blows each time, as it became clearer Ifi had no magical abilities.

Ekren hesitated. "Well, people like a wizard, you know? Heroic, or mysterious. We're—" she half-shrugged—"too big, too noisy. We have to practice together to make the magic come from the harmonies, okay? And we also have to be, well, *harmonious* together, or the magic doesn't happen. It takes consensus *and* music." Ekren looked over Ifi's head, clearly picturing something else. "And it's beautiful when we do it."

Ifi considered that. "It takes all of you to make magic?"

Ekren nodded slowly. "Well, most of us, at least. More than--" Ekren swallowed--"just Thisle and me."

"All right," Ifi said, voice turning brisk. "Let's get your family back to your ships before they're conscious. That way I've nothing to fear from you, and you--" Ifi waggled the spent pistol in Ekren's direction--"aren't in a position to disagree that you're in my debt for saving you from the sirens." *And*, she said silently to herself, *there's no chance I'll have to hurt you.*

Ekren choked. Kept choking. Ifi grew alarmed, reached a hand out––then realized the other woman was laughing. When she caught her breath, Ekren called, loud enough to be heard on the other ships, "Well, family? I see the clockmistress' point as well as the point of her pistol. And she seems a jolly one. So how about we take that one step further? Band together to fly on to Seffel?"

Nenet laughed, a dry sound. "I'm not coming down there to check out either of those points. You can have my vote."

Ekren looked at Thisle, but she was still asleep. "Obraham? Seht? Tahr? Ferna?"

No response from Obrahom but a new voice, sharp, called out. "I'm with Nenet. And here's my leg." Barefoot even at this altitude, Ifi saw. "Now leave me alone while I check on Tahr. He was on the stairs when he fell asleep."

"Ekren, why don't we just wait for folks to wake up?" A deeper voice also from the second pirate. "Then we can just finish what we were doing when the sirens arrived. Maybe there *are* valuable schematics down in the hold? Like Obrahom said?"

No, Ifi thought. *Get off my ship.* Her hands began to shake, and she forced them into her pockets.

She called up to Seht, "Which do you want? Your family members back or some schematics you probably can't even read?"

"Why do you think I can't?"

"Seht!" That sounded like Nenet. "We need to get the others back."

"But they'll wake up soon––"

Ifi interrupted, "But right now they are down here with me and my pistols." *My empty pistols*, she thought. And no heart to fire them.

"I'll come down and––"

Ifi pulled both pistols out and pivoted to point them at Ekren. "I wouldn't do that if I were you."

"Nenet, what about that ship gun?" Seht's voice muffled as he turned away from Ifi.

"No!" Ifi cried. She advanced on Ekren. Ekren's glance darted between Ifi's shaking hands and eyes. Ifi squeezed the handles of her empty pistols, her empty heart squeezed back. Even if she had loaded bullets, could she fire at another singing, living being today? "Please?" Ifi whispered.

"Seht," Ekren called, eyes locked with Ifi's. "Maybe we should try to trade for the schematics, if we really want them."

"Don't worry, Ekren, we'll think of some way to save you and the others––"

Nenet interrupted him, "Why not just use Ekren's suggestion?"

Seht sighed. "Have you looked in the holds recently? We barely have enough to get us to Seffel. We have nothing to trade."

"Of course you do." Everyone looked at Ifi in surprise when she spoke. "You can trade your promise not to hurt me. Or, your promise that I can join your band of pirates until Seffel, like Ekren said. In return, I'll send back your family."

"Why would you do that?" Nenet was clearly universal in the application of her skepticism.

Ifi scuffed a boot toe against the ship's deck. "There's a wizard. Probably chasing me." She cleared her throat. "I escaped and--"

"You'd do anything not to go back?" Ekren wasn't smiling. "Even become a pirate." An explanation, not a question.

Ifi nodded. "Even an efficient terror of the skies."

"Fine," Seht said, blowing out a bellyful of air.

Ekren asked, "Are only the four of us awake?"

"I think so," Seht called.

"Can you speak for the others?" Ifi asked.

"You can only promise us, Ekren," Nenet pointed out.

Ekren nodded her head. "We'll have to re-negotiate when the others wake up. Is it acceptable to make an agreement with just us for now?"

Ifi didn't think she could do anything else. They were closer to Seffel, but there was still a lot of sky left. "Yes." She lowered her arms, but they were still shaking. She pocketed the pistols.

"What's your name?" Seht called down. "We can't keep calling you the clockmistress." His blond head peered farther over the railing. "Unless that's a title?" He looked at Nenet. "Is that a title? Like nobility? I thought it was a vocation?"

Ekren rolled her eyes. "You'll need to untie me," she said to Ifi. Freed, she turned to Ifi and held out her hand, palm up. "Now, let's formalize this deal. Your name?"

"Sure," Ifi said. "My name is--"

"Ifigenia Glass, of the House of the Ransa." The voice was deep for a woman's and came from all around them. Ifi couldn't look up, as stiff with fear as a fully-wound mainspring, but Ekren did--and blanched.

"Dragon!" she screamed.

A deep thunk sounded from the first pirate ship; Ifi expelled a breath and softened enough to see Nenet positioning a long gun atop the railing. Ifi shook her head slightly. Most guns were too slow or too small a gauge to hit or harm a dragon.

"Ifigenia." Ifi was pretty sure even the pirates recognized that parental tone of voice. She looked up at the wizard riding the red dragon.

Cloak cast back, her black hair, pinned at the nape, flowed behind her like streamers. Or eels. Or hungry lightning. Ransaransa's eyes were the same sky-blue as Ifi's. One hand was wound through the dragon's hackamore. In the other, she lifted a palm-sized glass ball, pink like watered blood, which she used to focus her power.

Ifi hated that ball. Her gorge rose in her throat, jammed cogs blocking her breath. Instead, she looked to the dragon, whose wingspan was thrice the length of her airship. She blushed with guilt. Slowly, the dragon closed all three of its left eyelids, winking at her. Not angry. Still an ally.

"Mother, leave." Ifi put everything sturdy she could think of into her voice: struts, stabilizers, even the materials that flex and reshape, like canvas or the softer metals. She wasn't going back to being trapped in her room, or beaten, or having her clockworkers stolen and reprogrammed to hurt people. But to do that, she'd have to hurt people. She bit her lip.

Ransaransa watched Ifi a moment but didn't respond to her. Instead, the wizard turned to the pirates, bringing the dragon closer to Nenet's ship.

Ifi cut her off, "Don't bother. We've negotiated--"

"Then perhaps they will re-negotiate." Her mother always sounded gracious. She looked over the pirates, widening her smile.

The dragon rose and fell with the current, its smallwings flitting, its whiskers waving to taste everything. Scales flashed crimson, carmine, and fired clay in the sun as its long body undulated.

Ifi wondered whether the pirates knew that the bright silver patterns along its throat and belly were scars. She curved her hand into a claw shape, the dragon's own tell for pulling a prank. The spiral of her fingers was neither as elegant nor as strong as a mainspring. And even the most well-tempered mainsprings shattered under constant stress.

Shattered. Ifi raised her curved hand, her fist, to show the dragon. Her movement caught Ransaransa's attention.

Meeting her mother's eyes, Ifi threw a used pistol at the glass ball, shattering it in the wizard's grasp. Ransaransa screamed, long and agonizing like the screech of metal scraping against metal. Shards and pistol fell beneath the clouds.

Ifi startled as the dragon trumpeted, two pitches at once––Ekren gasped, and Seht belted out a harmonizing note––and then rolled to its side, sending Ransaransa down through the clouds after her magical ball.

Ifi bit her lip and closed her eyes.

The dragon's notes resolved from mournful to joyous. Ifi knew her own, un-silvered scars, would take longer to heal. Then a two-tone question. She opened her eyes.

The dragon watched her, a small thread of flame between their fangs. They curled their right claw, then wiggled their smallwings in farewell. They plunged below the cloud-line in the wizard's direction.

"Ifigenia?" Ekren's voice was soft and tentative.

"Just Ifi, please."

Ekren nodded. "Of course. Ifi. Do you––do you need a moment?"

Ifi swallowed. "No. Here's my hand. Let's seal this agreement."

Ekren reached out and set her palm above Ifi's. "To Seffel at least. We'll renegotiate there."

"Says who?" Obrahom called from down in Ifi's hold, using the flinty pirate voice from their first talk. A number of pirates shushed him at once, their scolding causing Thisle to groan and sit up.

Nenet's voice carried. "Didn't you see what she just did?"

"You mean, be a fearsome, efficient pirate?" Ifi asked, unable to meet Ekren's eyes. Ekren squeezed Ifi's hand gently.

In the distance, they heard the dragon sing out again. Seht responded, a long note that wound into a fast-moving sequence that to Ifi sounded like the changing pattern of pins on a rotating music box cylinder.

The rest of the pirates joined in: Obrahom with low, slow notes, Nenet and Thisle imitating the sharp strikes of a snare drum, Ekren slapping her hands together and ululating like a storm-cloud rumble, and Tahr, supported physically and vocally by Ferna, repeating Seht's melody at a pleasing interval.

Ifi breathed in time, holding tight to the image of her nearly-complete clockworker. She looked into the wind and blamed it for water in her eyes as she watched for Seffel to come into view.

Mary Alexandra Agner writes of dead women (pirates), (clockwork) telescopes, and (magical) secrets. Her science nonfiction, stories, and poetry appear in Sky & Telescope, Shenandoah, and Strange Horizons, respectively. She can be found online at http://www.pantoum.org.

Jack Among Wolves

by Wren Wallis

IT COULD NOT BE SAID that Captain Jack Valiant objected to illicit custom; what she did object to, strenuously, was being entered into such an arrangement without her foreknowledge and consent.

"It is my most ardent desire," the Captain said sotto voce to the great blond bear of a man at her shoulder, "that the portmaster should fling himself into the God-damned sea."

"He would have to go some way," her Chief Mate observed. "Better to desire he fling himself into the river, no?"

"Desire knows neither reason nor geography, Mr. Kuznetsov." The Captain stepped forward to address the trio waiting amongst their baggage on the gangway. "I am sorry; you could have the sigil of Black Bess herself and I'd still tell you to sod off. The Blackbird is a cargo vessel, neither obliged nor licensed to ferry passengers anywhere, much less to the bloody Sebiran border. As Mr. Hewlett damned well knows."

The governess, a neat, prim-lipped woman, had gone salt-white at the Captain's language, and now throttled her folded parasol in gentle fury or mortification. The grave-eyed child beside her only stared from beneath the enormous halo of her sun-hat.

"It is," the governess managed stiffly, "of direst urgency. This poor child's father lies upon death's threshold. She may never see him again. Yours is the only vessel at present liberty to enter Sebir—"

The Captain cut her off. "You are mistaken, madame. I'm at liberty to do no such thing, no more than any Ardish ship. The Sebiran border is close guarded at the best of times; since the assassination of Empress Elena, it is sealed. Christ with all His sorcerers couldn't get an Ardish ship into a Sebiran port just now."

"But the *portmaster*—"

"Can bugger a dog for a tuppence." The Captain folded her arms and gave the governess such a black-eyed glare as had sent customs-men packing in the past.

Governesses, however, are made of sterner stuff than customs-men, and this one merely lifted her obstinate chin.

The heretofore-silent third member of the traveling party exhaled a weary cloud of tobacco smoke. Mr. Kuznetsov, the Chief Mate, took a pointed step back.

"How much do you want?" the gentleman asked, and flicked the dog-end of his cigarette over the gangway rail, where the wind snatched and whisked it away.

"Mr. Black—" the governess protested.

He waved her off, his bespectacled gaze fixed on Jack.

"How much did you pay the portmaster for his seal on those passes?" she asked.

"That is not—" the governess attempted.

"One hundred fifty," the gentleman said. He drew a calfskin billfold from within his coat.

"Two hundred," said Jack. "Per person."

"Absurd!" the governess cried. "Six hundred! Better than the Bank Governor's salary! Who would *carry*—?"

But her traveling companion had already begun to count out that princely sum. He offered the notes crisply. "Do we understand one another, Captain Valiant?"

She plucked the notes from between his kid-gloved fingers and folded them into a pocket of her waistcoat. "Sufficiently. Were you seen coming up the tower?"

"By one or two early souls. We spoke of our impending departure for the Andalacian coast and asked at the platform below for directions to the mooring of the *Star of Tehrân*."

"Come aboard then and look sharp about it. Mr. Kuznetsov will see to your baggage. We'll bring you as far as Temsk. Not even my contacts can permit us farther, in light of the current situation."

As the governess ushered the child past, she reproached Jack, "Not even Christ with His sorcerers, is it?"

The Captain shrugged. "Christ didn't deal in cash."

THE DJINN-ROOM, THAT octagonal chamber at the ship's heart, held a darkly resinous whisper of myrrh and a buzzing tension like the approach of lightning on the air. The djinn in its central brazier was smoke given form, veins of flame writhing within. Its eyes were pits of brilliant fire.

Jack bowed to it, and for a moment it contemplated her, its electric regard raising the fine hairs on her arms. Then the blaze of its attention drifted indifferently away.

Jack skirted the brazier. Behind it, the djinneer stood frowning at an array of equations freshly chalked on her soot-blacked cedar table. "Donkeys within donkeys," she muttered in Atashi, and absently tucked a tendril of hair back beneath her headscarf, leaving a pale smudge of chalk on her smooth brown temple.

"Such vulgarity, Yasmin," Jack chided in the same tongue, and the djinneer looked up swiftly.

"Bah," she said, mingling relief and exasperation, and switched to Ardish. "You goose. What?"

"Are we ready to depart?"

"Of course, yes." Yasmin stepped aside to indicate the chalk-and-salt sigils elaborately diagrammed on the cedar planks of the chamber's floor behind her.

"Very good. I'll have Mr. Kuznetsov cast us off directly."

As Jack made to leave, though, the djinn rustled like embers in its nest of flame. Yasmin touched the spherical glass pendant at her throat. "Your new guests are liars," she translated.

"Of course they are," Jack agreed. "Honest men don't pay."

"Jack," the djinneer warned. "What if they're Melusian agents?"

"To what end? Why would the Astrologer King smuggle agents into *Sebir*, of all places? Sebir has no native sorcery, so surely no sympathy for his *puissantiste* cause. His war's with Queen Bess."

"Smuggle agents into a *closed* Sebir, in the wake of Empress Elena's assassination, in an *Ardish* ship? Imagine the mischief they might work, and the blame they might direct."

Jack weighed this. "It seems a great deal of trouble for Melusian agents to take." At the look on Yasmin's face, she relented. "I shall keep a weather eye on them, cousin. But I tell you, I caught no whiff of sorcery, Melusian or otherwise, on any of them." Her uncanny nose for magic had never yet led her false.

But abruptly she recalled Mr. Kuznetsov stepping back in distaste from the pungent cloud of the gentleman passenger's tobacco smoke, and it prickled at her like the djinn's regard.

"I shall keep a weather eye," she repeated thoughtfully.

BLACKBIRD cast off from Aldwych Aero-Port Tower just as the bells of St. Margery's began to sing six o'clock. The city below was still an expanse of darkness scattered with streetlamp constellations, but night was lifting like a curtain over the eastern sky to reveal a radiant swathe of gold-and-crimson beneath.

The djinn-ship maneuvered with practiced precision away from the tower before unfolding gleaming brass-jointed wings and rudders and turning its eager prow toward the rising light.

Belowdecks, a man dressed as an Ardish city gentleman smoked cigarettes and prowled his small cabin like a restless animal. A woman in the severe garb of a governess set aside on her narrow berth the elements of a lady's toilette and lifted out the false-bottom pouch from her carpetbag to check the documents within. And a white-faced child in an overlarge sun hat gazed out her porthole and gravely contemplated the coming dawn.

AT MIDDAY, JACK YIELDED the quarterdeck to a helmsman and descended to the main platform. Her passengers had emerged some time since — the gentleman first and rather hastily. He stood now with one hand clutching the forward starboard rail but as far from it as his reach allowed, and pointedly did not take in the view sliding past below. With his other hand, he smoked.

"Do you require a handkerchief, Mr. Black?" Jack enquired.

He turned to contemplate her approach above the wire rims of his spectacles. His eyes were a most extraordinary golden-amber hue, like whiskey held up to the light. "I have my own," he informed her dryly, and drew on his cigarette again.

"Some people do not take to air travel," Jack confided, leaning on the rail. "Even on a clear day, you know, a sudden wind may toss a vessel like thistledown."

His complexion took on a remarkable greenish cast, but he did not flinch and continued to weigh her in a steady gaze. At length he mused, "*Jack Valiant* is a peculiar sort of name for a woman such as yourself, is it not? Like an Ardish folk hero. A penny-dreadful name."

"Well, Penny Dreadful itself seemed too on-the-button. Pray tell me what do you mean, a woman such as yourself?"

"You are half-Atashi, are you not? Your father is —"

Jack drew herself upright; she was tall for a woman, and he not so for a man, and so they stood nearly nose to nose.

"I am *half* none of your damned business," Jack told him evenly, "and the other half spite. You know a deal of information for an ordinary gentleman."

Beneath the veiling tobacco, she noted, was no telltale whiff of enemy spellcraft. There was a distinctive scent, though, a familiar one—an impression of ice and pine, and some pleasantly animal odor—but it wasn't a magical smell, and she could not place its familiarity.

Mr. Black took a courteous step backward, his gaze untroubled. "I have wagered seven hundred fifty crowns thus far on this voyage," he said in his easy city drawl. "Do you not expect a financier to research his investments?"

Jack surveyed the man. His clothing was expensive in both cloth and cut, but worn casually: the tie-knot looser than strictly respectable, the coat-collar turned up. He was of no great height or breadth, fair-skinned, neat-bearded. His dark hair was, again, somewhat longer than might be expected of a gentleman, but on the whole the effect was that of a man with a deal of money and little regard for public opinion.

"Your *employer's* investments," she corrected.

"Naturally," he agreed. "My employer's investments. Though you will understand I have a personal stake—if I manage to convey his daughter to him before he passes, my employer has bequeathed me a substantial additional sum for the service."

"Pray remind me — what did you say your employer's business was in Sebir?"

"Chiefly in timber," Mr. Black answered, with an air of patient humor. "He made this most recent journey in hopes of broadening his interests to include a certain nickel mine."

"I thought Sebirans were terribly resistant to foreign meddling in their Empire."

The gentleman made a deprecating gesture. "The Empress— the *late* Empress, that is, Elena Verovna—was something of a reformer and had encouraged new openness to the West. My employer was ever quick to seize an opportunity." He shook his head. "God only knows what becomes of Western investment in the Empire now."

"It *is* odd about the timing. That he should be taken so ill on the heels of Empress Elena's assassination, as the borders closed."

The gentleman looked mildly taken aback. "Do you suggest some connection? Surely not."

"Well," said Jack, and clapped his shoulder heartily enough to give him a jolt. She took petty satisfaction in the panicked glance he threw at the rail. "Do enjoy the view."

AT THE OPPOSITE RAIL, the child stood with one hand in her governess's and watched the scuffed-slate plain of the sea far below. She was a dark-eyed little creature, with a thin, sallow face and a great mass of frizzy hair under that enormous hat. Jack had intended to pass the pair by, but the forlorn small figure exerted a sorrowful magnetism, and so the Captain paused.

"I am sorry to hear of your father's illness," Jack told her.

The child nodded uncertainly and then, at a nudge from the governess, dropped a curtsy. "Thank you," she said to her slippers.

There was some terrible misery writ plain on her, but it didn't to Jack much resemble *grief*. She stooped to the child's eye level. "Miss," she said as kindly as she knew how, "if you are in some other difficulty or danger—"

The governess made a startled sound and swept around, meaning to gather the girl back against her skirts.

The child did not yield, though; she stood steadfastly straight and lifted grave eyes to meet Jack's. "No, Captain Valiant," she said in a clear, piping voice. "But I am grateful for your concern." She hesitated and then added, more softly, "I have never been to Sebir. I am anxious, is all."

The governess squeezed the girl's small shoulders, and now the child subsided back against her.

Jack straightened. "Sebir has a peculiar reputation," she said, "because it guards its borders and its secrets closely. But there's no cause to fear the place. The good Mr. Kuznetsov, my Chief Mate, is Sebiran himself."

The girl nodded.

"Thank you, Captain Valiant," the governess said, by way of stiff dismissal. Jack bowed with elaborate mock courtesy before turning away.

THE STRANGE SHIP APPEARED as afternoon faded toward dusk. The watchman sighted it first, and halloo'ed from the spy's nest; Jack stepped to the rail and snapped out her spyglass to consider the black fleck against tattered cloud and colored sky.

"A ship," she affirmed. "Too distant for trouble, and it may yet alter course. But keep eyes on it."

As Jack turned away, the governess intercepted her. "Could it not be a bird? A *ballon*?"

"We'd have outpaced either swiftly, and neither holds so steady at apparent altitude. It is a ship."

The governess smoothed her skirts anxiously. "Not a hostile one, surely."

"Are you sure of it, indeed? I am reassured, madame," Jack replied. "For it is only that we fly a little-traversed route toward a destination no other ship should seek right now. The fact that there is another ship strikes me as peculiar indeed."

"Then what do you mean to do about it?"

"At present, nothing. It will have to be a damned sight closer for us to do anything useful."

WHEN NIGHT FELL, THE strange vessel vanished. Jack returned to her cousin in the djinn-room.

"We're changing our bearing," she told Yasmin. "Four points green. We'll come at the border more directly from the west and then bear straight north to Temsk. I need all the speed you can give me tonight."

"It's trouble, then," Yasmin said, already moving to stoke the brazier with charcoal.

"No sight of them. But I don't think they've changed course. I think they're flying dark."

"*Bother*," said Yasmin. She pushed up her sleeves. "I daresay we might conjure a fog as well, so long as we're over the water. Let them try to pursue a quarry they can't see either."

The djinn in its brazier rustled like laughter and wavered, casting strange shadows.

THE FOG WOULDN'T HOLD. Three times the djinneer raised it, and the shroud gathered. Three times a new wind from the south chased it clear again.

Nor was the wind a kindly one; it buffeted the Blackbird about, trying her wings and rudders, and set her crew scrambling to secure flyaway rigging and loose-rattling panels. Jack stalked the quarterdeck barking orders until her voice was rusted. The passengers huddled in their cabins.

Toward dawn, Yasmin mounted the steps to where the Captain paced. The djinneer was ashen with weariness. The wind whipped the tails of her knotted headscarf impishly. "They have a magician," she confirmed. "A strong one. Whoever they are, their aim is serious."

Jack had tasted the stale cathedral odor of incense on the wind half the night. "Melusian," she agreed.

The djinneer knit her brows. "But why? What is a minor Ardish cargo vessel to them?"

Jack stared into the blind, cloud-scudding black sky behind them. "At the rate they pursue us," she said grimly, "I would prefer to leave the why of it for another occasion."

DAWN'S FIRST GLIMMER revealed what Jack had dreaded. Not only was the strange ship still on a course to intercept, it had gained sky enough that even without her glass she could make out the stark outline of wings and rudders. "A Melusian *crécerelle*," she informed Yasmin, who still stood shivering beside her. "We're outgunned three to one."

Beneath them, land flowed past once more, the deep greens and stark greys of forest and scree; they closed fast with the Sebiran border, the Blackbird flying with all her fire.

"I don't understand," the djinneer gritted through chattering teeth. "Why such ardent pursuit?"

"Madame," said Mr. Kuznetsov diffidently, stepping onto the quarterdeck behind them. He was already gallantly shedding his greatcoat. "Please. It is quite a chill." He swept the coat over Yasmin, fairly swamping her in its expanse.

The djinneer nestled into its warmth and breathed a grateful sigh, as faint roses bloomed in her cheeks. "Most kind, Mr. Kuznetsov," she murmured.

Jack stared at them both.

Mr. Kuznetsov noted her regard first, and now he flushed as well. "Captain?"

"Step here," Jack commanded, and pointed to the planks at her feet. "Stand beside me."

Bemused and sheepish, he shuffled two steps to obey. Jack drew a deep breath of his presence.

Ice and distant pines. A warm, animal undertone.

But Sebirans have no native sorcery.

She turned her regard back toward the ship that trailed them like a carrion-crow. "Remind me," she said. "What was the name of your late Empress?"

"Elena Verovna," Mr. Kuznetsov answered promptly.

She shook her head, affecting a frown. "No, no. Yasmin, what was it?"

"He's correct," Yasmin said, puzzled. "It was Empress Elena."

"What did you call her, Mr. Kuznetsov?"

"Elena Verovna," he repeated. "But it is the same name, Captain. Sebirans use the matronym—"

"Yes." Jack turned on them triumphantly. "*Sebirans* use the matronym. Yet when I spoke to Mr. Black yesterday afternoon, he called her 'Elena Verovna.'"

"It could be," Yasmin offered, "that he's become accustomed, in his Sebiran dealings—"

Jack shook her head. "He smells like Mr. Kuznetsov. He *smells* like you."

Mr. Kuznetsov went chalk-white. "Christ God," he swore.

"What does it mean?" Yasmin demanded.

Jack folded her arms. "That ship doesn't pursue merely because we fly an Ardish flag. They pursue because we're smuggling Sebiran nationals back into Sebir, and it appears someone means to disrupt that homecoming."

WHEN MR. KUZNETSOV escorted Mr. Black to the quarterdeck, both men were set-jawed and silent. Mr. Kuznetsov was still pale and now perspiring, despite the other man's smaller size and genteel manner.

Mr. Black wore no spectacles now; the whiskey-bright eyes regarded Jack with sardonic amusement. "A fine alias after all," he drawled. "The *Jacks* of Ardish folktale are always clever."

"You will give me your identity. Bear in mind I'll put overboard a man who lies to me twice."

He lost a shade of color but held her gaze. "I understand your anger, Captain, but bear in mind that whatever else I may be, I am certainly your present ally. I am *aboard your ship* and would be considerably inconvenienced by its sinking."

"We're not going to sink," Jack informed him. "We're going to *land*. I'm going to run up the white and hand all three of you over, unless you explain."

He straightened and pressed his lips together but still made no answer.

There was a scuff on the stair. The girl ascended, her governess in tow.

"Captain Valiant," the child said in a thin, high, unsteady voice. "I beg your pardon for the ruse, and that we have endangered your good crew by it. This man is Aszer Chernovich Niyazov, of the *Imperatorskii Otdel' Volkov*—a captain of the Imperial Secret Police."

There was a moment's startled silence, and then Mr. Black—Captain Niyazov—sighed and reached into his waistcoat for a silver cigarette case. "Has anyone got a match?" he asked, dryly rhetorical.

"If he's a captain of the Imperial Secret Police," Jack said to the child, "would that make you—?"

"Grand Duchess Anna Elenovna," the child admitted. "Heir to the Imperial throne." Her small voice quivered as she said it, but her solemn gaze was steady.

"Well," Jack said, briefly rooted by revelation. She removed her hat and scrubbed a hand through her hair. "Honored, Your Highness. Perhaps you might do me the further honor of explaining what in the hundred holy names you're doing aboard my ship?"

"Her mother's antipathy for the *puissantistes* and her esteem for your Queen Elizabeth were no secret in the Imperial court," Captain Niyazov said. "The Astrologer King, I believe, took steps to keep Sebir out of your war, to ensure the Empire would not align itself with your queen's cause." He gestured with an unlit cigarette at the ship in pursuit. "*Takes* steps."

"I am a God-damned *smuggler*, begging Your Highness's pardon," Jack said. "I am not an agent of the Crown. Royal intrigues are well outside my sphere."

"This is the point in an Ardish story," Captain Niyazov observed, "when a Jack would do something clever."

"CAN WE BE CERTAIN THIS will work?" asked the anxious governess—a genuine governess, to Jack's surprise, one Miss Orlova by name—as Jack led them down the corridor.

"Certainty is for priests and mathematicians, madame, and I am neither." Jack glanced over her shoulder and saw the governess, white-faced and resolute, holding firmly to the little Grand Duchess's hand. It softened her somewhat. "But my djinneer *is* a mathematician. The timing will cut very fine, but I promise you the Melusians know very little of djinn-ships, and will never expect us to take such a risk."

THE SEBIRAN WILDERNESS at dawn was a place of secrets and shadows; small things rustled in the velvet darkness still gathered between ancient trees, and patient, predatory eyes kept watch from bough and burrow.

In the rose-streaked sky above, the tiny black silhouette of an airship appeared. A second, sleeker silhouette closed on it. From below, the pursuit was a dreamlike, silent shadow play.

The second ship gave a jolt that, from this vantage, looked like delicate hesitation. The ship in front bloomed a wreath of brilliant flame. A moment later, a distant thunder sounded.

The first ship hung for a breathless instant and then, trailing smoke, began to fall.

"WHAT IF IT DOESN'T return?" Captain Niyazov shouted above the whine-and-rattle of the falling ship. He and Miss Orlova had each braced themselves in a pair of the octagonal chamber's adjacent corners, the Grand Duchess wedged against the wall between them.

"It will!" Yasmin cried, clutching her glass-bauble pendant.

They all watched the empty brazier in the chamber's center.

Seconds rolled past. The ship's uncontrolled fall gathered momentum. Jack closed her eyes.

The whoosh was near-inaudible amid the racket of disaster, but it was followed by a bonfire roar and scorching heat on Jack's face. She opened her eyes.

The djinn flared like the rising sun in its brazier, too bright to look upon, and Jack flung up a hand to shield her eyes. She heard the governess cry out, and Yasmin's laughter.

"Ah, well done!" the djinneer cried in Atashi. "Well done, beloved!"

The djinn blazed with laughter of its own, sated on enemy incendiaries. Around them the clatter of free fall died as their wild plummet became a gently spiraling downward glide.

Captain Niyazov, still braced in the corner, one arm stretched protectively across the child, shook disheveled dark locks back from his eyes and looked to Jack. "And now?"

"Now," said Jack, and straightened shakily, "we lay the bait."

THE ARDISH SHIP LAY exposed on the clear slope of a rocky rise, just above the treeline. It listed gently to one side, and one of its fine brass-jointed wings had sheared off. Debris lay scattered in the grass.

A Melusian *crécerelle*, the *Demoiselle Victoire*, set down cautiously on the clear slope a little distance from the fallen *Blackbird*.

Nothing stirred aboard the wreck, and an ozone stink of burning hung in the air. The forest that fringed the lower part of the slope held breathlessly silent.

For a time the Melusian ship was silent as well, but at last she opened hatches and dropped ladders, and her soldiers boiled out toward the Ardish wreck.

They had ventured only partway across the field when Hell rose up around them.

UNDER COVER OF THE trees, Jack cried, "Fire!"

The Blackbird's crew ranged in shadow around her opened small-arms fire; hardly accurate at distance, but enough to sow panic. Enough to allow Mr. Kuznetsov and his comrades precious seconds to run out the *Blackbird's* starboard carronade and smash a jagged wound in the *crécerelle's* hull, whilst the two nine-pounders raked the approaching party with a brutal volley of grapeshot.

In the stunned, gun-muffled silence that followed, Jack screamed, "Forward!"

She and her party swarmed from the trees toward the bloodied Melusian survivors. Mr. Kuznetsov and his party spilled from the carefully staged wreck to close from the other side. Jack shot two men at pistol-range and paused to give a third, half-gutted by grapeshot, a mercy cut.

"Captain!" Mr. Kuznetsov bellowed, and Jack whirled to see a stained, disheveled blonde in the silver-ornamented coat of a Melusian *sorcière* raise a fistful of lightning, her expression dire.

A black shadow flowed across the field and leaped, bearing the *sorcière* down; when it lifted its head, Jack saw it was a great dark wolf, smoke-silver pelt shaded to black, jaws painted with blood. The *sorcière* sprawled unmoving at its feet.

The wolf regarded Jack with sardonic amusement. Its eyes were the golden-amber hue of whiskey held up to light.

"Well," Jack said when she had found her voice. "I am obliged, Captain."

The wolf grinned its canine grin and loped deeper into the fray.

WHEN IT WAS DONE, JACK left her crew scavenging the field and the Melusian ship, and went to see to Yasmin and the Sebirans.

Three of them waited in the clearing where she'd left them. Grand Duchess Anna Elenovna perched on a fallen log swinging her legs in the green cathedral forest light. Her governess stood with her. Yasmin stood some little distance away, clutching her glass pendant, which swirled with smoke and a glint of flame.

"It's done," Jack informed them, and looked about. "Where is Captain Niyazov?"

"I sent him to assist you," said the Grand Duchess, and stopped swinging her legs. "He seemed better used there."

"He's a shapeshifter."

"An *oboroten*," the child agreed. "All of the IOV are *oborotnii*. Everyone in the Imperial court is, really." She resumed swinging her legs. "You might want a word with your Mr. Kuznetsov about that, in fact."

"I might, in fact. But you aren't one," Jack guessed.

The girl shook her head mutely.

"And therein lies the trouble."

"Yes," Miss Orlova said quietly. "Sebir has its own faction sympathetic to the *puissantistes*. They opposed most of Elena Verovna's reforms. When it was evident that her daughter was not *oboroten* herself, Elena Verovna knew what they would make of it and arranged for her to be raised abroad, out of the court's eye. We had anticipated some—*resistance* to her investiture. Though I confess we had not thought our agitators would be so bold as to involve Melusin directly."

"And so now what happens?" Jack enquired.

"There will be some interval to see Her Highness settled on the throne," Miss Orlova said. "But I expect your queen will have her alliance with the Empire after all."

The Grand Duchess nodded.

"No," Jack said. "What happens *here*? Among us?"

"Captain Niyazov will have means of contacting some trustworthy IOV," said Miss Orlova. "They will get us all from here to Kyiv."

"And?" Jack prompted.

The governess knit her brows. "You have secured an international alliance and been paid *six hundred crowns*."

"And?"

Miss Orlova flushed indignantly. Beside her, the little Grand Duchess laughed. "We shall make additional provision, Captain," she promised.

The underbrush rustled, and Captain Niyazov himself emerged in his shirtsleeves, shaking back his disarranged hair and buttoning a cuff. "I did tell you, Miss Orlova," he chided. "She is a Jack. In Ardish tales, you must always wager on a Jack, even among wolves."

"JACK AMONG WOLVES" © 2018 by Wren Wallis

Wren Wallis lives in eastern Massachusetts with her husband and daughter and chickens. Her short fiction has appeared previously in Beneath Ceaseless Skies, Daily Science Fiction, Lackington's, and the Alliteration Ink anthology No Shit, There I Was. She can be found online at wrenwallis.com, and on Twitter way too often as @invisibleinkie.

Acknowledgements

MANY PEOPLE HELPED bring this collection to life, and it wouldn't have been possible without their efforts and assistance.

John:

First and foremost, I want to thank my tireless co-editors, Jo Miles and Mary Agner. They've been a part of every aspect of the anthology's production, from wrangling submissions to developmental editing, drafting a marketing plan, compiling the manuscript, and all the myriad other tasks involved in bringing *Skies of Wonder, Skies of Danger* to life. Turning the nascent idea of this book into reality couldn't have happened without them.

Thanks to our wonderful cover artist, the incredibly talented Gabriella Liv Eriksson, who appreciated both our vision and our limited budget, and created the amazing piece gracing our front cover. Gabriella was a splendid collaborator and we can't recommend her enough. You can find her work at *https://gabriellaliv.gallery*.

The inimitable Chris Wolfgang, another resident of the Isle of Write, was able to fit our work into her busy copy-editing schedule and helped put the final shine on it. She's a great editor, writer, and all-around terrific person. You can find her at chriswolfgang.com.

Thanks to MacAllister Stone and Valerie Valdes, who provided helpful advice on contracts and related matters, along with overall encouragement.

Thanks to the other members of the Isle of Write community, and all our other friends beyond the Isle, who supported and heartened us along the way.

Naturally, this collection would not exist without the talented writers who shared their stories. Thank you to Mary Agner, Hilary Bisenieks, Chelsea Counsell, Laura Davy, Amanda Hackwith, Tyler Hayes, Joshua Kidd, Jennifer "Macey" Mace, Kelly Rossmore, Clarissa Ryan, Tim Shea, Wren Wallis, and Fred Yost for entrusting your babies to us. I hope we've done them justice.

Finally, special thanks to my wife, Michelle Appel, who when approached with the idea of funding the project, not only consented but stepped in to handle some of the business aspects. That's in addition to all the usual dross that comes with being a writer's partner. She's talked me back from more than one ledge as I juggled *Skies of Wonder*, my day job, and my own writing. All love to you, hon.

Jo:

There are few things more gratifying than to start out with high expectations for a project, and then watching it exceed them all. That was the case with *Skies of Wonder*, and I couldn't have asked for a better first project as an editor.

So many people were involved in making this anthology a reality, and it was a true community effort. Thank you to all of the writers who submitted stories, for putting your faith in this project and for your patience with us, your editors. The entire Isle of Write community, from the contributing writers to our behind the scenes cheerleaders and advice-givers, has given this anthology constant and much-valued support.

Mary Agner, as my co-editor, has been a tireless warrior of e-book formatting, and her attention to detail throughout this process has kept us on track and made the anthology stronger.

None of this would have come about without John Appel, who took this idea and ran with it. I'm certain "that airship pirate wizard thing" would still be kicking around our conversations as an idea for the distant and hypothetical future if not for him. His endless hard work and enthusiasm was instrumental, and he's been the perfect captain for our little pirate ship.

And a particular thanks to Michelle Appel, who's believed in this project from the very beginning and has supported it in so many ways. I know I'm not the only Isle of Write member who's been grateful, many times, that Michelle is part of our community.

Last but certainly not least, thank you to my partner Nathan, who is my rock for everything writing-related, including this.

Mary:

Thank you, John, for letting me be a part of this adventure. Thank you, Jo, for sharing your marketing wisdom, your website know-how, and your suggestions on how to make my story better. You two have made this a rich, rewarding experience, and I'm grateful.

Editor Biographies

JOHN APPEL VOLUNTEERED *to jump out of planes before he'd ever been in one, which may explain why he volunteered to edit and publish this anthology. He's an SF writer by night and information risk pro by day. He enjoys both rum and swords but not at the same time. He tweets as @oldscout.*

JO MILES HAS BEEN ACCUSED *of being a wizard, but she'll never admit it. You can find her writing in Diabolical Plots, the Agents and Spies anthology, and Galileo's Theme Park. She tweets at @josmiles and lives in Maryland, where she is owned by two cats.*

MARY ALEXANDRA AGNER *occasionally edits and builds books.*

Made in the USA
Middletown, DE
18 November 2019

78978237R00125